DRIVER'S FLAT

Sonny Clanton

SP
Sabougla Press

DRIVER'S FLAT

This novel is a work of fiction. Any references to real events, businesses, organizations, and locales are intended only to give the fiction a sense of reality and authenticity. Any resemblance to actual persons, living or dead, is entirely coincidental.

Library of Congress Cataloging-in-Publication Data applied for

ISBN 978-1-7322644-1-0
Copyright© 2021 by Sonny Clanton
All Rights Reserved
First Edition

Cover Design by Brandi Doane McCann

SP
Sabougla Press

SONNY CLANTON

DRIVER'S FLAT

DRIVER'S FLAT
―――――――――――

DRIVER'S FLAT

I am part of all that I have met.
-Alfred, Lord Tennyson, "Ulysses"-

DRIVER'S FLAT

PART ONE

THE PRESENT - WINTER

DRIVER'S FLAT

DRIVER'S FLAT

CHAPTER 1

FLIMFLAM ALLEY

The winds, influenced by the leading edge of the polar vortex, plunged into the Deep South, reaching Cade County, Mississippi, on the Saturday afternoon before the Super Bowl. The temperature, within two hours, dropped from sixty-five degrees to freezing. The cold air blasted across the town square of Central City, taking trash, leaves, and anything that was not fastened through the south end of town to the river bridge, which was a mile away. Stores closed early. Business was slow because most patrons had not yet recovered from Christmas shopping.

When darkness fell, only Lola's Coffee Shop and two convenience stores remained open. Snowflakes, driven horizontally by the high winds, began to fall and accumulate. The slim, red-headed meteorologist at the Tupelo television station had predicted that no more than three inches would accumulate. He was usually correct.

As the night progressed, the air became visibly frosty. The muted glow from the street lights around the town square onto the air caused the gazebo in the center and the surrounding area to have a stunning appearance.

An occasional vehicle came onto the square leaving in another direction, its sound muffled in the snow. The wind rose even more, howling around the corners of buildings and down the alleys. The square was designed so that highways approached the center of each of its four sides. The traffic circled it in a counterclockwise fashion. Each corner had two alleys, perpendicular to each other, for traffic to exit.

On the northeast corner of the square sat Potshot's Poolroom, facing west. Adjacent to its north wall was Flimflam Alley which dropped sharply away from the square to the adjoining street. None of the other seven alleys was named.

Shortly after midnight, with the wind chill now in the lower teens, a figure moved furtively from the shadows at the back of the poolroom into Flimflam Alley. It moved slowly along the side of the building, searching along the way. The small male, dressed in an oversized, worn wool overcoat with a watch cap pulled over his ears, rummaged through a couple of garbage cans, muttering to himself all the while. He discarded most of the cans' contents, occasionally sticking a few treasures into his pocket: a half-eaten burger, a nail clipper, an empty green wine bottle and a soiled baseball cap. He stayed aware of his surroundings as he worked. His activity was not illegal, but he felt that rummaging was beneath his status and didn't want to be discovered.

The bent-over figure stiffened when the gleam from the headlights of a vehicle on the square hit the glass front of a store and then swung toward the alley entrance. He dived behind a nearby can as the car headed down the alley toward him.

The older Nissan stopped, the engine idling, and the window on the driver's side rolled down. Unaware that he was being watched from the cover of the garbage cans, the driver threw several objects onto the pavement and sped away. The observer watched the Nissan take a right on Cole Street and disappear. The car's left taillight was out.

As soon as the Nissan moved away, a handful of papers was scattered up and down the alley by the wind. The figure in the shadows didn't move for ten minutes, waiting for the coast to be clear.

Then the figure moved with curiosity toward one of the papers that was flattened against the poolroom wall and grabbed it. He stared! His toothless jaws opened, and he howled, "Hoowee! Hoowee!" He stuck the paper into his most secure pocket and scurried after the others.

CHAPTER 2
POTSHOT'S REQUEST

Central City's chief of police had retired, and the mayor had asked the sheriff to loan his chief deputy, Wade Sumrall, for the spot on a part-time basis until a replacement could be located and hired. Wade was willing to take on the duty. He already knew the three other policemen and had worked closely with them on various cases.

Wade was the chief deputy of Cade County, a veteran of the Korean War, having joined the Marine Corps when he was sixteen by lying about his age to be able to serve with his friend, Ellis Tiller. He had been in the bitter winter fighting at the time and place when the Chinese army joined the North Koreans. Wade had been a POW briefly, escaping and leading other Marines and soldiers to the American lines. His heroic efforts earned him the Navy Cross. Back home, he had never discussed his actions with anyone.

He was a muscular man with large hands and a stout torso. His thighs were thick as tree trunks. Even at his age, Wade was hard as nails. A deep scar, the result of fighting Chinese soldiers in hand-to-hand combat, jagged down the left side of his face. Women considered him handsome. He was well respected in the county; and as a result, crime hardly existed.

DRIVER'S FLAT

He dropped by city hall early on the Monday after the Super Bowl. The day was bitter and cold. The sky was gray and overcast. As Wade walked from his patrol car to the door, he shivered. Not all from the cold. The weather had brought back memories of the fighting in Korea. He was glad that was in his past.

He spoke to Melody Williams, the office manager, and to the town clerk. They smiled back. They were glad he was helping run the police force.

Melody said, "Wade, have some hot coffee and some of those sausage pinwheels my mom cooked this morning. Take your time, but when you get through, Potshot wants to see you at the poolroom."

"What about?" asked Wade.

"I dunno," said Melody. "He just said for you to stop by the poolroom the next chance you have. That there was no hurry."

Wade pondered the request as he ate a large pinwheel filled with home-cured, spicy sausage. Wade had a small farm connected to a large tract of woods and meadows where Potshot did a lot of quail hunting. Sometimes he would hunt a few hours with Potshot. His aging legs no longer held up to the strenuous walking that was required of quail hunting. Wade had grown up "bird" hunting, as it was called in the South, and had trained his own dogs. Of course, like most bird hunters, his dogs were also his pets. He would let them sleep by the fireplace in his house until his bedtime. His last dog, Dolly, a big female English pointer, had died a few years back at the age of twelve. His heart was not in training another dog, for he realized he didn't have too many years of hunting left. He didn't want to retire in the middle of a good dog's career.

He figured that Potshot wanted to talk about a hunt or ask permission to take someone else along on his next trip to the place. He would drop in after he made a patrol around town to see if anything was amiss. As he filled his large hands with the delicious pinwheels, he winked at Melody, "Don't get rid of your mom!"

Melody smiled as Wade left the room.

DRIVER'S FLAT

CHAPTER 3
THE POOLROOM

Norma Sue's Beauty Shop was located on the northeast corner of Central City's town square. Potshot's Poolroom was underneath the beauty shop, which is where an establishment which allowed the type of activity as it did, should be. Underground, out-of-sight of the honest, hard-working, church-going public. Away from the view of the youngsters of Central City. In fact, there was a sign at street level where a set of stairs dropped downward into what was characterized by the ladies of the Baptist church as a "Den of Iniquity," that read: *NO ONE UNDER FIFTEEN ADMITTED.*

Although the sign did not prohibit entry by a female, no woman in Central City had ever been down these stairs except Oscar Sappington's wife, Arlene, a tall, attractive blonde. She had appeared on her birthday in a violent rage looking for Oscar. Arlene had the reputation of being the meanest woman in town.

Oscar owned one of the two used car lots in Central City. Between vehicle sales, he spent most of his time chasing women. Arlene couldn't prove that he had girlfriends, but she suspected as much.

DRIVER'S FLAT

When Oscar had left home for work that morning, he was unusually nice to her and said he would have a surprise at lunch. Arlene, forever nosy, ransacked the house for a present. She found none, but she did discover a mail order catalog in a drawer of the night stand on his side of their bed. She thumbed through it. She noticed a page with imprints. Arlene glowed as she held the page up against the bedroom window to read the words. She knew that Oscar had placed the form on top of this page to write the order. Now she would find out what present she was going to get! Arlene moaned as she saw that Oscar had ordered a sexy, red bra with matching panties. She began to have fantasies. Then she shrieked a stream of cuss words. The size of the underwear was definitely not hers!

The occupants of the poolroom on that day heard Arlene's high heels clicking down the stairs, taking two steps at a time. Her heels were followed by a view of the rest of her body and a stream of foul words threatening Oscar, who wasn't there. By the time her head cleared the ceiling, the patrons had exited through the back door. The room was vacant except the owner and his helper. Not seeing Oscar, Arlene glared at them. The owner shrugged and gestured outward with his arms. Arlene's eyes locked in on the cut glass lamp hanging above the first snooker table, recognized it as a genuine Tiffany, gazed back at the owner in amazement, snorted, "Hmmmph!," and made a prompt exit.

The stairs to the poolroom were at the corner of Flimflam Alley which paralleled the north side of the beauty shop. To the right of the bottom of the stairs was a wall upon which shelves were constructed. The shelves housed a stock of snacks: boxes of candy bars, chewing gum, and cartons of cigarettes. An adjacent counter held the cash register and several glass jars that contained bags of peanuts, nabs, and large cookies that sold for a nickel each.

Just past the counter a couple of soft drink boxes were filled with chilled sodas. A row of game tables lined the right side of the room and a row of domino tables lined the opposite side.

The male social events in town originated in Potshot's. That is to say, before any young man picked up his date for the evening, he stopped by Potshot's to announce to all within hearing who his date was for the night. If the poolroom had not closed after he had taken his date home, he would return to bluster about his night.

The poolroom was open six days a week, from eight in the morning until ten o'clock at night except Friday and Saturday, when closing time was midnight. The ceiling was low; the lighting was dim. At the rear was a restroom which contained a long trough, since all the patrons were male. The original color of the trough was not known, but now it was basically green since it was rarely cleaned. There was one small lavatory and a paper towel rack fastened to the wall. An outside door opened to a grassy lot.

Around the game room was a scattering of spittoons, none of which seemed to have ever been emptied. Over the years, chewing tobacco had given way to snuff, and those users preferred to use empty drink bottles in which to expectorate.

The poolroom was owned by Potshot McCool, an outsider to Central City. Potshot grew up in Ohio and had played fullback for two years at Ohio State. He was a short, dark-haired man, and built like a bowling ball. His muscular legs were so big the insides of his thighs rubbed together when he walked. His career had come to an end in the fourth quarter against LSU in the Sugar Bowl. LSU's defensive end had delivered a devastating blow to his knee when Potshot went across the goal line on an off-tackle carry. During later surgery, a defect was discovered which prevented sufficient recovery. Potshot would never run the ball again.

While in the hospital he met Rhonda Thomas, a pretty, blonde physical therapist. Rhonda was from Central City. Upon graduating from Tulane's medical school in New Orleans, she had taken a job at Oshner Hospital, where Potshot had surgery. A romantic relationship developed, and Potshot transferred to Tulane to be closer to Rhonda. The romance turned into a marriage.

After obtaining a degree in general business, Potshot landed a job with a small stockbrokerage firm. At first, he worked at several trading desks but soon found his niche dealing in bonds. He had a gift for gab and was often the monthly sales leader for the firm. In his spare time, he engaged in day trading in puts and calls for himself. Slowly, he parlayed his savings into a seven-figure sum over a period of five years.

By this time, both Potshot and his wife had become weary of living in New Orleans. Crime had increased. The air was always steamy, and Rhonda had become homesick. They decided to relocate to Central City. Rhonda was hired by a local hospital to do the same work she had left in New Orleans. Potshot had nothing to do except play golf and hunt.

After a while, Potshot became bored, waking most mornings with idle time on his hands. He continued to dabble in the stock market and managed to make profits on small trades. He was patient and refrained from becoming greedy, which resulted in an increase in his wealth.

The owner of the town's only poolroom retired and offered to sell the business to Potshot, who was a regular snooker player there. Potshot bought the place, keeping on payroll the present manager, a crippled guy named Eck Roth, who was trustworthy and could be depended on to run the place for most of the day. Eck was as much as a fixture of the poolroom as the game tables. He had been there for twenty years, about the time the tables were bought.

Since the atmosphere of the poolroom was distinct, Potshot made no changes to the décor except to add the Tiffany lamp shade. It had cost him a bundle, but he had a fondness for colored lamps and had wanted to add a touch of class to this community man cave. He had been surprised when Arlene Sappington had obviously recognized the lamp's maker on her previous visit. Among his group of domino players, he doubted there was an art savant who could appreciate the level of taste the lamp added to the room.

When Wade came to the square in his patrol car around ten, the first thing he noticed was that all the parking spots near the poolroom were filled. Puzzled, he wondered what was going on because hardly anyone went to the poolroom on Monday morning. Norma Sue's Beauty Shop above was always closed on this day. He noticed a new, pink Cadillac parked near the entrance. The car had to belong to Henry Childs, who had the handle "The Musician."

Henry was a small, pale-skinned man with blondish brown hair. He was always tidily groomed, and his customary shirts were made of silk, size small. His favorite colors were pink, rose, and fuchsia. His pale hands were smooth, indicating he was accustomed to making a living dealing cards or shuffling papers of dubious origin.

Henry had earned his nickname from a hitch in Vietnam. He was the point man for a six-man LRP (Long Range Patrol) team which was assigned patrols in the rolling foothills near the north end of the A Shau Valley. His weapon of choice was a 12 gauge pump shotgun. Henry was so adept at racking its "slide" that his team members noticed and found the movement similar to that of a trombone player. Henry and team leader Sgt. Al "Mother" Rucker had each earned the Bronze Star for helping snatch a downed flyer hidden in the tall elephant grass near Camp Evans from the grasp of advancing NVA soldiers.

Henry had grown up locally and had spent his adult life in Memphis and Cade County, except for several hitches in federal prison on bookmaking convictions. Recently, he had received part of the Joab McMath estate for helping Earl Ray Fowler, a devisee of the McMath will, find the location of the McMath riches. The estate had been settled the past fall, whereupon Henry had left the area with his share. Today was his first appearance in Central City since last November.

As Wade parked against the inside curb of the square across from the theater, which was a few doors down from the poolroom, his cell phone rang. A few minutes were used to resolve an issue. As he put the phone on his seat, he noticed two men leave the poolroom and come to a pickup parked next to his car. He recognized Red and Early. Red, a tall, lanky guy was a regular at Lola's Coffee Shop on the north edge of town. He and his partner, Carter, had built a successful furniture manufacturing plant in Baxter. They had sold the business for a huge profit. At age fifty-five, all Red had to do was count his money, hang out at Lola's Coffee Shop, work crossword puzzles, and frequent the casinos at Tunica. Early Parker was a sidekick who was also retired. As they headed to Red's truck, Wade noticed the shorter Early taking two steps to Red's one.

They spied Wade and spoke. Wade asked, "What are you two birds up to?"

Red replied, "We're going to the Tunica casinos. I feel lucky!"

"I hope you come out better than last time," goaded Wade.

Red admitted, "Yeah. I made a fool out of myself."

Early chimed in with a smile, "He won $40,000 real quick at the blackjack table. Red gave me the money and told me to hold it. Not give it back to him no matter what he said because he wanted to take that amount home. He moved to another table and won over $100,000. Then he got careless and lost it. Red ran me down and asked for his stake. I refused. He asked why. I told him because of his instructions. He got haughty and said, 'It's my money and I want it!' I told him, 'You're a damn fool. Take it.'"

"What happened?" Wade asked.

Red ruefully admitted, "I lost it all!"

They all laughed.

"What's going on in the poolroom?" Wade asked. "Why the large crowd on Monday morning?"

Red replied, "Everybody is down there watching the Musician shoot snooker."

"I didn't know the Musician could shoot snooker," said Wade.

"He can't," answered Red.

Baffled, Wade asked, "Then what's the deal?"

Early spoke, "It's the huge ring he's wearing! I've never seen anything like it! People can't take their eyes off the ring! The crowd is not watching his shots, just the movement of his right hand!"

Wade laughed, "Is Henry soaking up all that attention?"

Early replied, "Hell, yes! He planned this. He called me and Red last night and told us to be at the poolroom this morning. That he was going to show the local rednecks something that they had never seen!"

Wade wished them luck as they left. He decided to come back later after the poolroom crowd had dissipated. In the meantime, he called the police chief at Baxter, a town in the north end of the county, and the police chief of Vena, another town east of Central City in the south end of the county, for a crime update. Neither responded. Wade figured they were on patrol.

CHAPTER 4
GUS

The noon hour had passed before Wade had a chance to visit Potshot's. The morning crowd was gone, so he was able to park by Henry's Cadillac at the entrance. The only people in the room were Eck, Potshot, and the Musician, who was idly dropping balls in the pockets of the first snooker table under the light of the multi-colored Tiffany shade.

Wade stopped in his tracks, dumbfounded. On Henry's right ring finger was the most dazzling piece of jewelry he had ever seen! He couldn't take his eyes off it as Henry moved around the table placing shots.

Wade commanded, "Henry, come over and let me look at that ring." Henry placed his hand on the snack counter under the light of the colored lamp.

The flashy object was a huge 14 karat gold butterfly ring. Wide, double wings spread away from the insect's body, which was raised above the base ring and mounted on a small golden log. The wings, body, and head were covered in diamonds! Henry said there were forty-eight of them. The ring glittered in the light as Henry turned it for all to see each facet. The Musician was gloating at the attention his ring was attracting!

And it was as if the butterfly was also conscious of the scrutiny and responded by twinkling even more.

Henry said the ring was made to his design and that it took his jeweler multiple attempts to get it right. Wade asked who made it, but Henry refused to say.

Wade asked, "How long have you had the ring?"

"Got it Saturday. This is the first day I have worn it in public."

Wade knew Henry had planned for this: an audience. He was also wearing a gold bracelet with the words *The Musician* spelled out in diamonds. On another finger he wore a ring mounted with a 5-carat, European-cut diamond. Wade knew that this stone came from Henry's share of a stash of diamonds found in Joab McMath's estate.

Wade complimented Henry's jewelry and then asked Potshot, "What did you need to see me about?"

Potshot answered, "It's about what Gus showed up with when I opened this morning."

Arley Gus Bowen was the poolroom sweeper and general flunky. He was a short, balding man of indeterminate age. His gums were toothless, and he was continually working his jaws in a chewing motion. His trousers were hitched high above his waist. He had a booming voice. Gus had difficulty handling alcohol and became arrogant when drunk. Very few knew exactly when he had arrived in Central City.

He had no family and boarded in a small room in an old hotel in town. The door to his room opened to the back of the building, and Gus could come and go as he pleased. He also worked for other businesses in town as needed, including sweeping the floors of the Tram Theater, located on street level and just four doors away from Norma Sue's Beauty Shop. His clothes and food were donated by church ladies and civic groups. Gus was the town pet and the unofficial high school football team mascot. He was slightly retarded and the butt of many jokes, some of which were crude.

Wade asked, "What did he show up with?"

"Gus usually comes in late on Mondays. But today he was already at the door waiting for me to open," said Potshot. "He was shivering in the cold. He scurried inside and turned up the gas heaters. Then he grabbed a pack of nabs and a Pepsi."

"So?" asked Wade.

"Well, I normally charge what he gets to eat and drink in here during the week and take it out of his pay on Saturday night. But, he eagerly pulled out a $100 bill and demanded change," said Potshot.

Eck nodded, for he had followed Potshot in from the street and had heard the conversation.

Wade perked up. "I've never seen him with a large bill. Where did he get it?" he asked.

"That's why I called you," said Potshot. "He wouldn't tell me. He said it was none of my business and that there was plenty more where that one came from. He stuck his chest out and berated me for thinking that he was without means."

Eck agreed, "That's right. Gus started strutting around the room talking down to us like he was King Tut or something!"

"Yeah, from what all he said you could get the idea that he was the beneficiary of a trust fund," said Potshot.

Wade became suspicious. "Do you think he has stolen some money?"

Eck said, "I doubt it. I've known him for many years. There's never been any talk around town about Gus being dishonest."

Potshot added, "I agree. I wouldn't let him work here if he was a thief. But I've never seen him with a bill larger than a twenty."

Wade asked, "Where is Gus?"

Potshot laughed. "He left here saying he was going to buy a pair of expensive new shoes and have the shoe shop put taps on the heels. Gus said he was going to walk by the poolroom at night on the concrete sidewalk at the top of the stairs and make sparks fly bright enough that folks at the back domino table could see them!"

Wade, still laughing, said, "I'll run him down and see what I can find out."

As Wade walked up the stairs to the street, he realized that the Musician had listened intently to every word of the conversation without participating. Had he picked up on a clue about the money?

CHAPTER 5
MONEY IN THE ROAD

The Caraway family lived on a small farm a few miles outside Central City on a gravel road. Their neighbors were scattered along the road in both directions from their house. Mrs. Caraway was bustling around the kitchen preparing a hot lunch. School was out for the winter holidays, and her husband and son had left before daylight to go duck hunting on nearby Gallatin Lake. It was the middle of the morning, and her daughters, Holley and Anna, were just now getting out of bed. Suddenly, their mother realized that no one had gone to the mailbox at the end of the driveway since Saturday. She was expecting a tin of shelled pecans from a store in the Delta.

She said, "Anna, put on your coat and gloves and go see if my pecans are in the mailbox."

Anna whined, "Mom, it's too cold."

The mother said firmly, "Go get the mail and take Lucy with you. She hasn't been outside this morning."

Anna moaned, for she knew Lucy would want to sniff all around the yard. The toy dachshund loved to take a lot of time with this ritual, and Anna would be freezing by the time Lucy got through.

DRIVER'S FLAT

Anna was shivering as she opened the door of the mailbox to see the expected package of pecans. Her eyes bugged when she saw what was under the tin: a stack of $100 bills!

Before Wade had a chance to find Gus, he got a call from his dispatcher, Inez Roberts.

"Wade, something odd is going on in the county. Lois Howard, the librarian over at Baxter just called here. This morning, Mr. Jon David Knox was at her desk checking out a book. When she went to take the card out of its pocket, she discovered nine $100 bills stuffed inside. The sheriff wants you to look at them."

"Okay," agreed Wade.

"And, there's more. We got a visit from the Vena police chief."

"What about?"

"He brought in a dozen $100 bills that he had taken away from some migrant workers at Wright's potato shed on the north edge of Vena. The chief said when they opened the door to a van this morning to load a shipment of sweet potatoes, the bills were laying on the floor. The Vena police got involved because a fight broke out among the greedy workers."

Wade asked, "Did he get all the bills?"

"The chief thinks he did. He searched all the men and found no more."

Wade said, "This is very strange. Gus showed up at the poolroom this morning with one."

Inez said, "The news of those money finds have hit the coffee shops already. Jon David Knox had made a bee-line to Lola's. He was the center of attention and retold his story to every latecomer. Jon David was hot because the librarian wouldn't let him keep the money, which he claimed was his."

"How was Lois able to keep him at bay?"

"Oh, she said since he hadn't yet signed the check-out card, the money still belonged to the library, or its rightful owner."

Wade laughed.

He didn't particularly care for Jon David. Neither did anyone else. Sixty-year-old, chubby Jon David Knox sold accident insurance for a national company to poor people in the county. He was suspected of cheating his customers by pocketing their premiums. His sales job was part-time, so he had a slew of time to hang around the courthouse, the barber shop, any event that provided a free meal, or Lola's Coffee Shop, to run his mouth. Jon David contributed nonsense to every subject broached. He was largely supported by his wife, who worked as a clerk at the local telephone company in Central City. Since he upbraided her habitually in public, Jon David was loathed by every woman in town.

Jon David lived in Central City but lately had been a regular patron of the library in Baxter. His incessant rude and obnoxious behavior toward the staff of the library in Central City had caused him to be banned. The joke around town was that the only other time the library had invoked a ban was when a volume of *Elmer Gantry* had arrived in 1927. The local Methodists had been accused of engineering that ban because the book's shady, central character was a member of their own denomination.

Lola's was one of three coffee shops in Central City. Actually, it was a stand-alone shop while the other two were located in convenience stores.

Lola's Coffee Shop served breakfast, lunches, menu items after the noon hour, and lots of coffee. Her shop faced the west side of the highway where it left the north limits of Central City. A sprawling, gravel parking lot wrapped around the front and one side of the shop. Teenagers and college students filled the lot on weekends and kept the carhops busy. On the busiest nights, a parking space at Lola's could be more valuable than a free meal. The youths passed their time cruising the town square, making multiple trips to check out the activity at Lola's, and returning the mile to the square.

Inside the shop, five plywood booths lined the wall to the right of the door. A long community table filled the center of the room with a counter to the left. Nine stools lined the linoleum-covered counter. In the back, a dozen tables seated four diners each. This spot generated a sense of privacy while the community area was generally boisterous.

This morning, Reese Jones, Jon David Knox, Andy Morgan, and Mayor Todd West sat at the community table. They all were regular customers at Lola's. They usually started their conversation with gossip, but today the truth was the hot topic. The news of so many $100 bills turning up recently in strange places was being kicked around.

Todd said, "I wonder how much money has been found that hasn't been reported?"

"I bet a bunch," responded Jon David.

"You got that right!" said Little Ben Weaver, a quail dog trainer, who had just entered the shop. Ben was a wiry man, weathered from many years of working outside. He had a perpetual squint from looking into the face of the glaring sun and blowing wind. He was sometimes mistaken for an Indian. Ben worked for a construction company during summers and trained dogs for quail hunting in the fall and winter. He also was a regular at Lola's. "This county is full of opportunists, just waiting for good fortune to fall into their laps," he reasoned.

They were all curious about where this money was coming from, and each had his own ideas.

"I think there has been a bank robbery somewhere and the robbers are afraid some of the bills are marked," said Todd.

Reese Jones, the local undertaker, said, "I bet it's more of Mr. Joab McMath's money that didn't get found when his estate was probated."

Joab McMath was a frugal old man who had died recently. His will had been hotly contested. A small amount of his money had been found in the county, but a large fortune had been located out west.

Jon David blurted, "Yeah! That's it. Compared to what they found out in Texas, he should have had a lot here where he could get to it."

"Well, our guard unit just got back from Iraq for the second time. You know, the first time the news was in the papers about other soldiers finding all kinds of American and foreign money in those countryside palaces," added Andy, a local insurance agent.

"Yeah, but I heard that when units were sent home, the military searched them and their equipment very thoroughly. I doubt our guys were able to bring any back on the first tour," said the mayor.

Little Ben interjected, "They could have stashed money somewhere to bring back later when security would be relaxed."

Jon David questioned, "But how would they know they would be sent back after the first tour?"

"They wouldn't. But, it doesn't take a rocket scientist to figure that the odds of returning to Iraq would be high. Anyway, nothing ventured, nothing gained," replied Little Ben.

"Listen to Socrates!" exclaimed Reese.

They all laughed. Reese thought to himself, I'll bet Little Ben suspects more than he is telling. He usually holds his cards close to his chest. It wouldn't be the first time that Ben had contributed to a puzzle being solved.

Little Ben added, "Or the bills could be part of drug money going back to Mexico that someone got their hands on. They could be scattering those bills to see if the law would get suspicious. If their drug dog didn't hit on the bills, they would know they weren't tainted."

Jon David replied, "Yep. Could be. There are tons of 18-wheelers coming through this town every day. They could be hauling money or drugs for all we know. But I haven't heard of one being stolen lately."

Reese replied, "Dunce, a truck could be stolen somewhere else and brought here to be hidden by a local. Nobody wouldn't even know about it."

DRIVER'S FLAT

CHAPTER 6
LOU BERTHA'S TIP

A week later, the morning meeting of the Cade County Sheriff's Office in Poston, the county seat, started at 9:00 sharp. Sheriff Grady Powers was sitting behind the large walnut desk. He was a short, portly man who always wore a suit or a sport jacket and hat.

Around the room was Chief Deputy Wade Sumrall; bald and burly Deputy Jack Early; swarthy Sammy Baker, who resembled a linebacker; and 30-year-old, enjoyable, Sally Ryder, a brunette who still had her trim figure from her college days. They were deep in thought as they viewed the different stacks of newly-found money that were heaped on Sally's desk. Law enforcement had taken the bills found by Gus, the library, the Caraways, and Wright's potato shed, and the finders of the bills were given a receipt.

Grady had asked County Attorney Tina Allred what should be done about the money. Tina remembered that the first chapter in her property case book in law school had been about lost property.

She laughed as she informed Grady, "The rule on found money is 'Finders keepers, losers weepers.' It actually belongs

DRIVER'S FLAT

to the true owners if they left it somewhere with the intent to retrieve it later."

"How much later?" asked Grady.

"There's no time limit. You would just have to look at the facts of each instance and make a common-sense judgment if someone showed up to make a claim," replied Tina.

"Well, I don't think anyone leaving money in a book or a mailbox would be expecting it to be there when they came back for it."

"Agreed," said Tina. "I'll run an ad in the paper giving a potential claimant thirty days to make a claim for the money. If someone does, we will take it from there."

"What if no one comes forward?"

"Give it back to each person who found the money."

Grady scowled. "I expect we'll be dragged into court by Jon David on his find. I intend to give that money to the library. They need it more than he does."

Tina laughed.

Jack Early announced, "All this money being found is causing problems around the county. The mail carriers are getting complaints from households about finding their mailbox lids being left open to the weather by night-riders. Apparently, people are riding around and checking the boxes for more money."

"Yeah," replied Sally. "The librarian at Central City said she had a rush of patrons at her place when the news broke about Jon David's find in Baxter. The people were pushing and shoving each other to get to her stacks. According to her, every book she had was taken from the shelves and searched. They weren't all put back either, leaving a mess."

Then Sally added, "It also didn't help that our county missionary found five $100 bills in a book in the library!"

Wade gawked, "You mean he was in that frenzy?"

Sally chortled. "The librarian said he was first in line!"

The sheriff asked, "What was the name of the book?"

Sally answered, "Of all titles, *Evil Money*."

Her disclosure caused Chief Deputy Wade to grin. "That is an appropriate title for hidden money, and it's ironic that a man of the cloth would pick out that book."

Jack asked, "What is the book about?"

Wade replied, "Money laundering." He read most nights if he wasn't on duty.

The sheriff pondered, "I wonder who is leaving this money around and why?"

A conversation began about a likely origin. A range of sources was concocted: a bank robbery, drug money, a theft from someone's illegal stash, a secret Santa.

Sheriff Powers instructed, "Y'all keep thinking about this. So far this activity hasn't been illegal, but we don't need any more civil unrest to develop. I'm going over to Baxter to check on the Santa angle."

Grady put on his hat and left the office.

Wade turned to the others. "The drug slant seems to be the most likely. It could have been stolen from a dealer somewhere, and it's being thrown around to see if it'll be checked for authenticity."

Jack said, "Yeah. If it's from a bank robbery, the idea would be for the bills to make their way to a bank which would detect any markings."

"I wonder if a drug plane carrying laundered money has crashed around here?" asked Sally.

"We've had some storms lately, and a plane could have gone down during darkness without anyone knowing," replied Jack.

"Or a hijacked trailer loaded with drugs and money may be hidden locally," remarked Wade.

DRIVER'S FLAT

The deputies began to prepare various reports and make telephone calls. While they were busy, the door opened and Lou Bertha Eason walked in with a large box in her hands and cheerily said, "Mawn-in!"

Lou Bertha was an ample black woman about seventy-five years of age. She was wearing her usual tattered dress, a white cloth wrapped around her head, and worn shoes on her feet. Her lower lip was pooched out by a generous dip of Garrett snuff. She was a jovial, likeable person who was a friend to everyone she met.

Wade welcomed her, "Have a seat, Lou Bertha. Haven't seen you in a while." Lou Bertha owned forty acres of land at Sabougla, a village in the southwest part of Cade County, just off the highway that led to Gallatin. She lived in a small, white, wood-framed house. Most of her land was devoted to pasture, where she had a dozen cows. A truck patch from which she sold vegetables in the summer was located in one corner of her property.

"I've been busy rounding up empty beer cans from them joints across the county line," she replied. Cade County was dry, so the county-line honky tonks were heavily patronized by Cade County citizens, causing a heavy build-up of empties in their trash bins.

She continued, "Aluminum prices are high right now. I'm striking while the iron is hot. I'm in with all them joints, and I'm trying to keep it that way."

Wade grinned. Lou Bertha was a savvy businesswoman. She was always busy buying and selling, or trading. For income, she sold vegetables, the few calves she raised, sweet potato slips, light bulbs, and anything that had a profit margin. She also baby-sat, hauled folks who didn't have a vehicle to town, and loaned out money. Although she drove an old car and had frugal ways, Wade had inadvertently found out that she had a large savings account at a local bank.

"What brings you by?" asked Wade.

"I just fried some half-moon muscadine pies this morning from the fruit I gots in my freezer. And I've got a good price on them." She flipped the box top open, and a delicious aroma filled the room.

"Oh, man!" exclaimed Jack. "How many do you have?"

"Two dozen."

"We'll take all of them."

The deputies shelled out cash to the smiling Lou Bertha.

Jack bit into one, rolled his eyes, and exclaimed, "I'm in heaven!"

The others agreed through mouthfuls of pie.

Lou Bertha instructed, "Now, don't y'all eat them up. Be sure to take some home to your folks."

The deputies meekly nodded in agreement.

As Lou Bertha stuffed the bills into her purse, she looked over at the stacks of the found money on the desk and said, "I see y'all are washing yo money now."

Silence filled the room. Sally asked, "Why do you say that?"

"I can smell the detergent from over here. It's Oxydol, the same brand I been using for years. It's hard to find," said Lou Bertha as she waddled out of the room.

"I knew it!" exclaimed Sally. "Whoever is leaving that money around suspects it's tainted by drugs!"

"Yeah. They're expecting the law to test the bills. If drugs aren't detected, they know their laundry operation works," chimed in Jack.

Wade laughed. "That takes the term 'laundered money' to a different level."

DRIVER'S FLAT

CHAPTER 7
GUS' REVELATION

Wade dropped in at Jamie's Lunch Counter, an extension of one of the convenience stores in Central City. The owner had added a room to one end of his building and had made a door to connect it to the eatery. The room consisted of a long counter with stools and six tables. The menu was limited to soups and sandwiches, which were served quickly.

When Wade entered, he spied Gus at a corner table facing the door. Gus had stuffed a paper towel into his buttoned collar for a chin-wiper. He was noisily eating a bowl of chili with his toothless gums, spilling juice all over his bib in the process. Wade could see that when Gus was finished with his meal, there would be a chili line on his shirt.

Wade paid for his sandwich. As Jamie took the cash, he picked out a $100 bill from the register, showed it to Wade, and silently nodded toward Gus. Wade sauntered over and asked, "Who bought your lunch, Gus?"

Working his gums furiously, he loudly retorted, "I did, you dummy!"

Wade sniggered, "It's not payday yet."

"I don't need to wait for payday no more," said Gus as he puffed out his chest. "I've got plenty of money!"

Wade slid a chair out and sat down. "Where did you get money, Gus? Have you robbed a bank?"

Gus shifted his eyes away from Wade's hard stare and refused to answer.

Again, Wade pressed, "Did you steal it? You look kinda sneaky."

Gus became defensive. "Now, Wade, you know I'm an honest man. I made this money on the stock market!"

Wade bit his lip. He knew this kind of talk came from the poolroom. Gus looked in awe to certain braggarts at the domino tables and was prone to mimic their claimed exploits. "Gus, honest men don't lie. 'Fess up. Be a man."

Gus was silent for a while. Wade could see his thinking wheels spinning furiously. Gus furtively looked around the room. Then he lowered his head and leaned into Wade and stated, "I found some $100 bills in Flimflam Alley that cold night when it was snowing."

"How many?"

"Twenty."

Wade leaned back in astonishment, "How did they get there?"

"I don't know. It was after midnight, and I was raiding the garbage cans. A car came off the square into the alley and stopped about half-way down. I hid in the shadows. The driver rolled down his window and threw papers out. After he left, I went out and found a $100 bill. The wind was blowing more all around. I got busy trying to catch them before they blew away. Man, that was hard work!"

"Did you recognize the driver or the car?"

"Nah. You know, I hardly get out of the poolroom or the theater, so I don't know who drives what."

"Do you remember what kind of car it was?"

"Nah. It was just old. Oh! The back light on the driver's side was out."

DRIVER'S FLAT

Wade got up to leave but paused, "Did you get all the money?"

"I don't think so," said Gus. "I saw at least one bill fly across the street. I went back just after daylight to search, but I didn't find another one."

Gus grabbed Wade's hand and requested intently, "Mr. Wade, you won't tell how I got this money, will you?"

Wade winked. "Gus, as far as I'm concerned you made that money on the stock market. Buying and selling shares of McDonald's."

Gus breathed a sign of relief.

He squeezed Wade's hand even more and pleaded childishly, "Please, Mr. Wade, you won't tell that I raid garbage cans, will you?"

Wade slapped Gus on the back and replied, "Man to man, Gus, what's said in Jamie's, stays in Jamie's."

CHAPTER 8
THE POOR BOX

Thirty-year-old Mollie Carver was parked in front of the Farm-to-Fork Supermarket in Vena, a small town on the east side of Cade County. It was 6:30 on Tuesday night. The store closed at 7:00. Her car heater was running, but she still shivered because she was sick with a migraine and a cold that she hadn't been able to shake. Mollie's four-year-old son, Harry, was in his safety seat behind her, pleading to go into the store with his big sister.

Because of the way she felt, Mollie had sent her daughter, Gracie, into the store to buy some food. Gracie was ten and was mature. She always tagged along with her mother while grocery shopping and knew the location of the foods that the store put on sale. Mollie was broke and could only afford sale items, whatever they might be. Tears came into her eyes as she watched Gracie through the plate-glass store window. Gracie pulled a cart out of the line and proudly moved down an aisle in the nearly vacant store.

Mollie was a frail, dark-haired woman. Her husband had died unexpectedly two years ago from a bout with the flu. They lived on a small farm outside Vena and had farmed sweet potatoes. She had worked with him in the fields which he inherited from his parents. He had also leased acreage from neighbors, and they were just beginning to get on their feet when the disaster struck. Mollie was forced to rent her farm to a local farmer and had to find part-time work in town. After the debts and bills were paid, there was little left. Last fall's rent income had already been spent.

Gracie clutched a $10 bill and her mother's shopping list. Her mother had instructed her not to buy any of the items unless they were on sale. First, she put a dozen eggs, a loaf of bread, and a 12-pack of instant oatmeal into her cart. Then she headed to the back of the store where a huge box held bargain items. This was where her mother bought most of their food.

She paused and anxiously looked around to see if anyone was watching her. Her innocence had been shattered at school last week. Some of her mean classmates had taunted her about her mother having to buy their food from the "Poor Box" in the market. The girls laughed at her. She was hurt, and she had not known how to reply. Gracie had been so quiet that night her mother noticed. But Gracie wouldn't tell her mom what was bothering her. Until that incident, Gracie had thought it was fun helping her mom sort through all the cans and bags in the big box.

All alone at the "Poor Box," Gracie rummaged through the jumbled contents, finding most of the things on her list. Before a can or bag was put into the cart, Gracie checked the expiration dates as her mother had taught her. She added a large jar of peanut butter with a torn label, bent cans of tuna, and dusty bags of dried beans. She filled out the order with Ramen noodles, which she was sick of eating.

As she was digging to the bottom, she noticed with joy a box of Lucky Charms, her favorite cereal. Its sides were bulging. Gracie wistfully handled the package. Her mother wouldn't buy cereal because of the cost, and the only time she had this treat was on rare visits to her grandmother who lived

DRIVER'S FLAT

in Tupelo. Hesitating, she added the Lucky Charms to the cart and removed a package of noodles, which was on sale for fifty cents. The cereal box had no price sticker, but because of its condition, Gracie hoped it would be cheap.

Satisfied with her selections, she moved to the check-out manned by Mrs. Hamilton, a teacher in her school. Mrs. Hamilton was related to the owner, Mr. Keeton, and filled in when he was short of help.

She spoke cheerily to Gracie, "Why, hello! Where is your mom?"

"She's out in the car with Harry. She has a headache," replied Gracie.

"Well, you did a good job with your shopping," bragged Mrs. Hamilton as she took the items out of the cart and began to scan the prices.

Gracie placed the $10 bill on the counter and watched the screen apprehensively as the total became larger. The cereal box was the last to be scanned. Mrs. Hamilton turned the box all around looking for the price. She could tell from its bulges that it was definitely on sale. She, as well as many others in the Vena community, knew of this family's financial plight.

"Do you have any more money?" Mrs. Hamilton asked Gracie.

"No, ma'am," said Gracie with pleading eyes, as her small body noticeably tensed. "We won't have any more money until mom gets paid on Saturday."

Mrs. Hamilton saw that after the sales tax was considered, only $.50 remained out of the $10 bill. She turned her head away and thoughtfully pulled a group of stapled, blank price sheets from a booklet. "Here it is. Fifty cents," smiled the checker. "I'll bet that could never happen again."

When they got home, Gracie took the groceries into the kitchen while her mother led Harry to his room. When Mollie came back to the kitchen, Gracie was taking the groceries from the bags, feeling a warm glow from being able to help her sick mother. When she took the Lucky Charms out, her mother snapped, "I've told you we can't have cereal. You need milk with it. Which I just can't afford!"

Gracie was crestfallen. She whimpered, "Mom! I'm so sorry. I'm so sorry." She ran to her room and dived under the covers. Mollie sat down at the breakfast table, put her head into her arms, and began to sob because of how sick she was and how broke she was and how she had hurt Gracie's feelings. Gracie was trying so hard to be a big girl.

After a while she straightened up, went back to Gracie's room, and hugged her. "Gracie, you did a good job tonight helping me. I shouldn't have scolded you. I found money that I had forgotten about in one of my dresser drawers. Enough to buy milk. I'll run and get a small carton before y'all wake up in the morning."

She held onto Gracie until the young girl relaxed and went to sleep. Mollie crept silently down the hall to her bed in a small bedroom. She was unable to sleep, thinking of her dire circumstances. On several occasions, she had leaned on her mother to borrow money for Gracie's school lunches. She felt she had worn out her welcome and refused to ask for more. Mollie was struggling to get by. There was no room for car trouble or an appliance breakdown. Then, as on most nights, she cried her pillow wet with the worries of how she was going to feed her children.

Early Wednesday morning, Mollie put on her robe and slippers and headed to the store to buy the milk. She would have to use some of the money that was meant for buying her migraine medicine. She would just have to tough it out at work the rest of the week.

Back at the house, Mollie was bustling around the kitchen as the children were happily opening the box of Lucky Charms. She was startled when Harry squalled, "Mom, this ain't Lucky Charms!" She wheeled to see Gracie looking into the box with huge eyes and a dropped jaw.

Mollie moved to the table and peered into the box. It was stuffed full of bundles of money! She pulled one out to see that it contained $20 bills! She sat down, trembling.

CHAPTER 9
RUNNING THE TABLE

Sheriff Grady Powers pulled into an empty parking space in front of Side Pockets, a poolroom on the town square of Baxter near the Skuna River. Another cold, gray day with very little traffic circling the square. He went inside and found that he was the only occupant. Kelly, the owner's youngest son, was behind the counter at the back, grilling a few burgers for a call-in order. Grady made his way past the pool tables and took a corner seat. Kelly spoke and placed a mug of hot coffee in front of Grady.

"Where's your dad?" asked Grady.

"Bank. Back in fifteen," replied Kelly, a man of few words.

Grady sipped the coffee and looked around the room in silence. He reflected that this poolroom had a character different from the one in Central City. Side Pockets had a grill to cook burgers, fries, and hot sandwiches. The front windows were so clouded with stale cigarette smoke that vision was blocked. The glass hadn't been washed since the Korean War! The tables, though, were of exceptional quality for a small town poolroom. Grady knew why. It was rumored that the owner allowed wagers on the pool games and that this establishment was a favorite stop for hustlers who bet large sums on the games.

Some blown-up, dusty pictures in wooden frames hung high on the south wall. Pictures of William Ottis Hurst, a local who had played fullback at Ole Miss during the Vaught dynasty; the first sawmill in town; Danny Caldwell, another local, who had been a hoopster at Ole Miss around 1960; a county American Legion baseball team that had advanced to a state tournament; and the previous owner's oldest son standing by Willie Mosconi at a pool table in the student union on the Mississippi State University campus in 1964.

Mosconi had been world champion of pocket billiards fifteen times. He had retired because of health reasons, and the Brunswick Corporation had hired him to put on exhibitions at places that hosted their tables. Because the college bought thirty of their pool and snooker tables for the new student union building, Brunswick sent Willie to Starkville to put on an exhibition.

Grady smiled as he recalled the story of what had happened. Well-known Willie arrived at 10:00 on campus in Starkville on a Tuesday morning in October. The walls of the gaming room were already lined with students, many of whom had cut classes to see Willie shoot. The students quickly noticed that Willie, a small, balding man, was in a surly mood. He uncased his mother-of-pearl "Balabushka" cue from a leather case and fitted the two pieces together. Without speaking to anyone, he then went from table to table, taking a few shots on each one as the spectators watched in silence. Willie was trying to select the best one for his exhibition. He came back to the first table, and despite being the agent for Brunswick unexpectedly announced to the crowd, "None of these tables are worth a damn!" The remark brought snickers from the boys.

Willie looked the crowd over and asked, "Is there any one of you boys that can shoot a decent game of nine-ball?"

Two of the boys present were really good, and the camp of each began to chant, "Ray, Ray, Ray", and "George Mart, George Mart, George Mart."

Ray was pushed forward by his buddies. Willie invited him to shoot first. Ray had grown up in Side Pockets back home and was nearly unbeatable. He shot four racks before he missed a ball. Willie took over and ran the table ten times before he told Ray, "Son, you need to sit down. Nobody can beat me." Willie held the world record of 526 straight shots.

Willie then proceeded to make trick shots, all of which thoroughly entertained the crowd. He was renowned for making the trick shot for Paul Newman in *The Hustler*. He duplicated the feat at the end of his exhibition and received a lengthy round of applause from his audience. When he posed with Ray for a picture, he finally smiled!

Burl Hardin, the current owner, walked in followed by a blast of cold air. He shivered as he went around the counter and placed his bank bag on a shelf underneath. He grabbed a cup of hot coffee and took a seat next to Grady.

"What brings you to Baxter?" he asked.

"For info I can't get elsewhere," replied Grady.

Burl looked away. This was payback. He was certain Grady knew about his back room poker games and the hustlers' bets on pool games, of which the house got a cut. The sheriff's office had never bothered him, which resulted in their holding markers on him.

Grady said, "I'm trying to find out why all this money is showing up in my county."

"Everybody over here in Baxter has heard the news. My customers are speculating about this," said Burl.

"Do you think a secret Santa is doing this?"

"Nah," said Burl. "You know the famous Secret Santa was from here."

A young guy from Baxter, down on his luck, had left the small town some years ago for the Midwest. Eventually, he built a fortune in telecommunication. Remembering his many earlier years of poverty, he began to anonymously give many strangers a $100 bill each during the Christmas season. The regular holiday donations caused a national sensation and were covered by all the television networks.

"Anyway," continued Burl, "that Santa died a few years ago. And Christmas is already gone."

Grady asked, "Could this be a copy-cat?"

"I doubt it. There is too much stealth involved with this money being dumped."

Three customers came inside to the counter and put in orders. Burl got up to help Kelly. After Burl got some burgers frying on the grill, he placed Grady's ticket for the coffee by his mug. On it was written, "See Ed."

CHAPTER 10
THE CHAMPIONSHIP GAME

Fifteen minutes before classes were to start at Central City High School on a February Monday morning, Deputy Wade Sumrall pulled into the back parking lot. As he strolled through the rows of cars, he noticed several of the students quickly toss lit cigarettes. He chuckled.

He entered the building and made his way to the office of Principal Phil Mayo. Mr. Mayo had called at daylight this morning and, with a sense of urgency, had asked Wade to drop by for a meeting. The school secretary greeted him with a warm smile and said that Mr. Mayo was impatiently waiting.

Wade went inside and took a seat. Mr. Mayo said, "Wade, I'm in a tight and need your help."

"Why, sure," replied Wade. "What's the problem?"

"It's about the Central City girls' basketball team winning the North Mississippi tournament down at Louisville Saturday night."

Wade frowned. He had been scouting for speckled trout the past weekend at Biloxi in advance of the season's opening and had only learned about the victory this morning. "How could winning a tournament be a problem?" Wade asked. "Did you pay off the referee?"

DRIVER'S FLAT

Phil laughed. "No. We won fair and square. But the president of the school board of West Utica, who we beat, doesn't think so. After the game, the West Utica fans caused quite a commotion in the stands, and this guy egged them on. He strode across the court and got up in faces shaking his finger saying, 'I'm turning y'all in to the state office on Monday.' He was very angry and tried to fight, but their coach grabbed his arm and dragged him away!"

"Who is their board president?" Wade asked.

"I've found out that his name is Danny Heiskell. He owns a furniture plant in Utica County. He works 1,000 employees and is one of the most influential businessmen in that county."

Wade pondered, "Well, what caused the West Utica fans to get so upset? It was just a ball game."

Phil replied, "Let me explain. We beat them three times by one point each time in the regular season. In the North Mississippi Tournament, after winning one elimination game, we then beat West Utica by the score of 48-39."

Phil continued, "Their coach, Bobby Deakle, then faced a dilemma. West Utica was a smaller school than us and could only afford one basketball coach. It just so happened that Bobby's boys' team was in their North Mississippi tournament at Pontotoc, a town eighty-five miles away. Both his girls' and boys' teams were playing the next night. He chose to coach the boys' game because they had the best chance to go further in tournament play. Bobby asked Chip Griffin, our coach, to coach his girls. We had already played each other many times, so Chip was familiar with the skills of the West Utica girls. With Chip at the helm, the West Utica girls easily defeated Shannon 41-29, making him a hero in the eyes of the West Utica supporters, but not with the disgruntled Shannon fans who filled the gym with loud, nasty remarks."

Wade acknowledged, "That figures."

DRIVER'S FLAT

Phil continued, "West Utica's glow of victory soon faded. They had to face us Saturday night for the championship, and their coach was back. We beat them in a hard-fought game. And guess by how much? One point! They went ahead 50-49 with five seconds left. Coach Chip called timeout. With his girls huddled around him, Chip explained a final play. The timeout ended and three players ran down court to stand under the goal. Coach Deakle put his tallest players around them to prevent a court-length pass. At the whistle, strong-armed June Parker threw the ball to unguarded Betty Wilson at mid-court. Betty swirled and lofted a two-handed set shot. As the ball arced toward the gym's rafters, the buzzer sounded. The crowd became silent, their eyes locked on the brown sphere as it descended and knocked the bottom out of the net."

Wade asked, "What happened then?"

"Pandemonium broke out. Their fans accused Coach Chip of cheating because he knew the West Utica playbook from coaching their team to a win three nights before. Their school board member, Mr. Heiskell, said it was unethical for a coach to coach two different teams in the same tournament."

Wade laughed. "Talk about sore losers!"

"Yeah!" said Phil. "But I don't need to have a complaint lodged that would cause us not to go to the state tournament this weekend. Do you know anyone in Utica County who might get that guy to back off?"

"I've known the sheriff in that county for years," said Wade. "He and some of his friends rent a cabin near the backwater of Gallatin Lake to crappie fish each year. He always invites me and Sheriff Powers to their fish fries."

"Could you call him and see if he could help us?" asked Phil.

"Sure," replied Wade. "Let me see what I can do."

Phil pleaded, "And do it this morning, if you will."

DRIVER'S FLAT

"By the way," Wade asked over his shoulder as he got up to leave, "did the Shannon school folks threaten to turn you in?"

Phil made a face. "No. Some of their supporters who hang around that truck stop up there told Coach Chip that they got beat too bad to whine. But if they ever caught him stopping in their town, they were going to whip his butt!"

CHAPTER 11
THE BANK ROBBERY

After lunch, Wade made his way back to Poston, the county seat in the center of the county. He went to Sheriff Grady Powers' office and passed on Mr. Mayo's request. The two decided it would be best if the sheriff made the call.

As Wade sat across the desk, Sheriff Powers dialed his friend, Mose Hankins, who had been the sheriff of Utica County for several terms. Mose, a former highway patrolman, was a stocky, sandy-haired man with a receding hair line. He was reaching retirement to the dismay of his citizens. His supporters were apprehensive of the future change in office since they were well satisfied with Mose.

Mose was in his office in the county seat of New Alton. After an exchange of pleasantries, Sheriff Powers explained Principal Mayo's problem. Sheriff Hankins laughed. "Hey, don't worry about that. Danny has cooled down. He was going to carry out his threat of turning y'all in until the brackets for the state tournament came out over the weekend. It was pointed out to him that West Utica, as second seed from the North, was paired against a team whose two best players were injured in an auto wreck on their way home Saturday night. They won't be able to play next week."

Grady let out a sigh of relief. "So he thinks West Utica can go further in tournament play with that match-up?"

"Yeah," replied Mose. "Danny said that piece of luck lets us live to fight another day!"

Mose changed the subject. "What's going on down there? We've heard about all that money that's been found in strange places!"

Grady coughed. "We don't have a handle on that, yet. Nearly every day, my staff and I discuss where that money could be coming from and why."

"Do you think it's coming from an illegal source?" asked Mose.

"One of our strongest suspicions is that it's from a bank robbery somewhere. The robbers might be worrying that the bills are marked. They may be lying low, knowing that those discarded bills will make their way into the banking system. If no alarm is sounded, then they will know the loot is clean."

"Have you had any of the found bills examined by your local bank?" Mose asked.

"Yeah. They weren't marked. But others could be," replied Grady.

Mose said, "We had a bank robbery nearby just before Christmas. The federal agent, Fred Roberts, who worked the case, said it was only the second one in Mississippi within the past year."

"Where was the other one?" asked Grady.

"Columbus," replied Mose. "It happened about two weeks before ours. The FBI agent laughed about that one!"

"Why?" Grady asked.

"It was funny to him about how they caught the robbers. According to him, these three young dudes decided to rob a branch bank on the east side of town that's located in a busy shopping center occupied by a supermarket and lots of retail stores. Their plan was for the one named Curtis to park his car

DRIVER'S FLAT

near the bank among other vehicles. That guy would leave the car there with the trunk lid unlocked and then mingle with shoppers. He was on the sidewalk as his two accomplices robbed the bank and fled by his car, throwing the bag containing the cash into the trunk. Immediately, police cars, fire trucks, and ambulances arrived. Curtis, along with a growing crowd of spectators, watched the excitement. When all responders finally left, Curtis fastened his trunk lid and drove away, suspected by no one."

"Did the other two get away?" asked Sheriff Powers.

"Yeah. The police couldn't find any witnesses who noticed them."

"But you said they were caught quickly?"

Mose sniggered. "Crime doesn't pay. Curtis met the other two at an abandoned house, as planned. They divided the $30,000 from the bag they had thrown into the car trunk. But then it all fell apart."

"How so?"

"One of the dudes couldn't resist showing off his sudden wealth and gave his girlfriend two $100 bills. The next morning, she went into the same branch that was robbed and asked a teller to break them into smaller bills. Guess what? The bills happened to be from the teller's marked stack. The police were called, and she was arrested and taken to the station to be questioned."

Grady exclaimed, "Tell me more!"

"Well, one of the other guys bought the morning paper to read about the bank robbery. He was reading with pleasure about how the police had no clue of who did it; how the robbers had worn non-descript clothing; and how the two had kept their heads at an impossible angle for the camera to get any meaningful picture. Then he absorbed the disclosure of how $65,000 had been taken. Not $30,000!"

Grady replied, "I bet that went over well!"

DRIVER'S FLAT

"Like a lead balloon!" Mose replied. "He got his buddy and they chased Curtis down to a corner bar. They accused him of raking $35,000 off the top before they split the balance. A heated argument developed that ended in a physical brawl. The police were called, and the three were arrested. The girlfriend had already squealed on them."

"Did they recover any of the money?" asked Sheriff Powers.

"Yeah. All of it. They hadn't had time to start spending any."

"Well, I can eliminate that loot as a source of where our found bills are coming from. Tell me about your robbery."

Mose answered, "The robbery here was at Driver's Flat, the village just over the line in Tippah County."

"Why were you the one to work it?" asked Grady.

"The village doesn't have a police department, and most of my deputies were already nearby. The annual Christmas event in Driver's Flat is held just south of town and spills over into my county. About 700,000 colored lights and 700 decorative inflatables stretch along a mile of the highway. Every year thousands of visitors show up. Many officers are needed for traffic control for a few days. About ten o'clock on Saturday night, one of my deputies, George Blake, was sent into the village for refreshments. He was not familiar with the streets and made a wrong turn looking for the store. This street turned off the highway between a small motel and the bank. He first noticed that none of the street lights were working. Then Blake noticed there were no lights in the motel or the adjacent houses." Sheriff Hankins enjoyed telling the story.

"As Blake moved along slowly, he sensed all his wheels bump over an object that felt like a traffic recorder. Puzzled as to why the cars on that narrow street needed to be counted, he stopped his SUV and got out. He spied an oxygen line and an acetylene line stretched across the street. They had been covered with loose dirt. He followed them through a row of shrubs into the motel parking lot. The lines were hooked to a commercial, mobile welder. He turned and followed them in the other direction, and they led him behind the bank building."

Mose seemed very serious as he described, "Blake jumped into his SUV and drove around the bank. He stopped the vehicle squarely toward the building with the headlights on high beam. As he exited, the back door of the bank opened, and a figure in dark clothing appeared holding a pump shotgun."

He continued, "Blake, the deputy, screeched in a high-pitched voice, 'Halt! I'm the law!'"

Mose said that the figure snarled, "I know who you are," and noisily racked the shotgun.

He continued, "Blake dived into his SUV, put it in reverse, and stomped the accelerator. The shotgun blasted his windshield out just as the SUV backed down into a deep gully at the rear of the parking lot and stopped with a thud, the headlights glaring into the tops of the nearby trees."

"What happened next?" Grady excitedly asked.

"Blake wasn't hurt. That special glass we had installed in our vehicles saved him. He got on the radio and alerted the others. The heavy traffic at the Christmas event delayed their arrival. In the meantime, the robbers got away. But he got off three wild shots with his pistol in the direction of a fleeing van."

"Wow!"

"Hey, Grady. A call has come in about a bad wreck. I need to go. I don't think any money from our bank is showing up in your county. Talk to Fred Roberts, the FBI agent in Oxford. He can fill you in on the details. Good to hear from you."

Grady answered, "Okay. Fred is coming by this week to look at our bills. I've known him for years. He worked at a bank in Memphis before he got on with the FBI. He went to school with my niece at Ole Miss. They dated some. I was hoping they would match up, but it never happened."

DRIVER'S FLAT

CHAPTER 12
THE JUNIOR AUDITOR

Fred Roberts, an FBI agent stationed in Oxford, was not in a good mood when he drove into the parking lot of the Cade County Sheriff's Office in Poston. On the way down from Oxford, he had been delayed. He was talking on his cell phone and absent-mindedly followed the flow of traffic toward Water Valley for a few miles before he discovered his mistake. The morning rush hour made time seem like forever before he could get turned around. He decided to take some back roads to reach Highway 9W, the route from Oxford to Poston located in the center of Cade County. He exited onto a county paved road which, to his dismay, ended at a work site where a bridge was out. No signs to that effect had been posted along the way. He had to backtrack five miles to Providence Road, an isolated gravel road. In a dark mood, he continued his journey.

He soon hit the highway and was delayed even more by an overturned, loaded log truck which was blocking traffic. His final delay was caused by the traffic lights being out in the town of Baxter.

Fred was wilted as he walked into Sheriff Powers' office. A forty-five-minute trip had turned into two hours. He was uncomfortable in any meeting when he didn't arrive on time.

DRIVER'S FLAT

Sally Ryder, the female deputy, greeted him and showed the bills from the different finders. Fred examined each carefully. He punched the serial numbers into a site on his laptop to see if they were linked to the Driver's Flat bank robbery. Negative. He frowned.

Grady had walked in while Fred was working. He said, "I'm frowning, too. We can't get a lead on this money."

Fred said, "That bank robbery was strange. The federal bank examiners came in and did an audit because of the heist. A large shipment of new bills had arrived the day before. That's all they took. None of your bills match the numbers on the Federal Reserve list. About $20,000 in older bills in the vault were not bothered. They cut open a few lockboxes, but it looked like they were interrupted."

"Did you find out what they got out of the boxes?" asked Sally.

"We interviewed all the owners of the opened boxes that we could find, and to our surprise, the only thing taken was a baseball autographed by Stan Musial. Some of the boxes contained several thousand dollars in cash and expensive jewelry."

"Sounds like a weird robbery," replied Wade Sumrall who had just finished bringing a prisoner to the jail.

Fred replied, "Yep, considering what the bank examiner stumbled upon."

"What?" asked Sheriff Powers, straightening up in his chair with interest.

"Driver's Flat is not far north of Interstate 22. The bank is small. They only have the bank president, two tellers, and a secretary who fills in when the bank lobby gets crowded. One teller operates the drive-in window. Because of its size, the bank only gets cursory audits by the state examiner whose department is understaffed. The federal bank examiners had a newly hired auditor with them. Boy, talk about a nerd. His name was Stacy Dweeb."

"No way!" exclaimed Sally, as the men guffawed.

"Oh, yes." replied Fred. "And there's more. He wore thick black-framed glasses, his shirttail was out, his fly was unzipped, and he had dried egg on his face from breakfast!"

The sheriff's crew laughed as they imagined Dweeb's appearance.

"But," Fred continued, "that fool stumbled upon something that is a mystery."

"What?" asked Wade.

"Without being told, Stacy took it upon himself to determine when the vault door was opened. As if that would make a difference. He hooked his laptop into the security system of the bank and identified the exact moment the door was breached. He found more."

"What else could he find?" asked Wade again.

"Stacy ran a printout of the times the door was opened and closed for the past year. His boss sneered and told Stacy that the information was useless. Stacy slunk to a corner and studied the list. After a few minutes, he called for me to come over and look at it. Stacy had noticed that the vault door had been opened a couple of weekends a month. The door only stayed open about fifteen minutes on each occasion."

Sheriff Powers abruptly stood up and questioned, "What was going on?"

"We don't know," said Fred.

"What did the bank manager say?"

"That's the problem. We can't interview him. He and his wife were in Jackson when the robbery happened. Sheriff Hankins called him to report the robbery. On his way up I-55, he ran off the road into Arkabutla Lake in the middle of the night and was killed."

"He drowned?" asked Sally.

DRIVER'S FLAT

"No. The trooper on the scene said that the car came to rest in waist-deep water about thirty yards from the lake edge. Neither Craig Synott nor his wife, Doris, was injured. But she was terrified. Since Craig didn't know how deep the water was between the car and the edge, he told his wife to stay and he would go to the road and flag a vehicle for help."

"Did he make it?" asked Sally.

"Yes," said Fred. "But a motorist reported that he staggered in front of an 18-wheeler and got splattered. Travelers began stopping to assist. No one knew about the car being out in the lake until Doris was heard screaming. She was soon rescued."

Sheriff Powers asked, "What progress have y'all made about the vault being entered? Was money taken at any of these times?"

"Nothing is missing. The examiners went over the books with a fine-toothed comb. They are in perfect balance. We have interviewed all the bank employees. They are as mystified about the weekend visits as we are. Plus, the state auditors never look at times the vault is opened. Sort of moot if no valuables ever disappear."

Fred added, "This issue is on our back burner. We have a lot going on right now and are shorthanded. Sheriff, could your office help us? Of course, we wouldn't surrender jurisdiction. We know you are a close friend of Sheriff Hankins. There is no police department in Driver's Flat. It's too small. Apart from that, we never interviewed the widow who is now staying with her aunt in Central City. There was no reason, since she didn't work in the bank. Could you talk to her?"

Grady agreed, "Sure. I'll have Wade, my chief deputy, do some detective work." Grady pointed to the man at his side.

Wade Sumrall laughed, "Like I don't have enough to do as it is."

"I'll have my office send you our reports and the contact info on Doris Synott," said Fred.

Wade stated, "I'm curious about how the robbers got into the bank."

Fred scowled and concluded, "This robbery was well planned. The thieves knew that everyone in the village would be at the Christmas event. They parked a welder against the shrubs at the motel next door and ran the lines across the street to the back of the bank. The lines were covered with dirt to conceal them from passing motorists. We don't know how many robbers there were. There had to be several: a lookout, two or three to work inside, and a driver. We think the cash had already been hauled away by the time the robbery was discovered. You know, Deputy George Blake reported the lights were out in the area."

Fred continued with the mystery, "Tom, the lineman with the power company, reported that he found a log chain thrown across the lines in the area of the bank. That shorted out power and neutralized the bank's alarm system. We don't yet know how the back door was bypassed. After they got into the building, they cut the vault door open with a thermic torch. They also used the torch to open the lockboxes. Of course, Deputy Blake discovered something amiss, but he was observed by their lookout who must have alerted the ones on the inside with his cell phone."

"What about the welder? Did you trace it?" asked Wade.

"Yeah. It had been stolen in Memphis the day before. We found no prints or DNA. Those guys were professionals."

CHAPTER 13
DORIS SYNOTT

A few days later, Deputy Sumrall and Deputy Sally Ryder called on Arneda Young, the aunt of the newly widowed Doris Synott. Arneda had let her stay for a while. Doris was a shapely brunette in her late twenties. She and her husband had not yet started a family. She was still on bereavement leave from her third-grade teaching position in New Alton.

Arneda left to go to a club meeting. Wade welcomed the privacy. Wade and Sally expressed their condolences to the young widow. They listened patiently as she tearfully told about Craig's death, the funeral, their life together, their life plans, and her uncertain future.

Then Wade asked, "How long had y'all been in Driver's Flat?"

"Oh, about three years. Craig started with a bank in downtown Memphis right after college. He soon realized that he had no future there. To get a promotion, you had to either be in the upper social circle in Memphis or have old family money in the bank. Lots of it. Craig didn't fit into any of that. He had a friend, Lewis Carty, who owned a nearby stock brokerage firm. They lunched together several times a week. When Craig admitted that he was in a dead-end job, Lewis recommended that Craig should get on with a smaller bank. He then sent Craig to David Black, an acquaintance who owned an employment service. David, with lots of contacts in North Mississippi, located an opening in the Driver's Flat bank, which was locally owned. Craig was interviewed by the bank's board and was hired."

Sally asked, "How did y'all like living in Driver's Flat?"

"We loved it," responded Doris. "Both of us were from small towns. I grew up in Tiptonville, Tennessee, and Craig was raised in Lodi, Mississippi. It was like coming home! We both had become weary of the Memphis rush-hour traffic."

Wade coughed nervously. "Would you mind telling me about the wreck?"

"That was the most horrible thing that has ever happened to me," Doris sniffed. "I was on the front seat asleep. Craig was driving fast on the interstate. It was late, so he thought there wouldn't be any cops out. I don't know what happened. He must have gone to sleep. Sheriff Mose had called him about the robbery, and Craig was in a rush to get home. It was about one a.m. The noise of the car going off the road woke me. It was bouncing off the shoulder. I screamed! Water hit the windshield, and the car stopped out in the lake. I was so scared. I didn't know where we were. It happened so fast. Craig said we were in Arkabutla Lake."

"Exactly what did Craig say?" asked Wade.

"He noticed the car was sitting in shallow water. He told me to stay there, and he would get out to the interstate and flag a car for help. Shortly, I heard tires screeching and a truck stopped. Then lots of cars stopped. I started yelling for help. Two men waded out to the car and carried me to the highway. That's when I found out about Craig. Can't believe he stepped in front of a truck."

Doris began to sob. Sally moved over to the couch and put her arms around the widow's jerking shoulders.

DRIVER'S FLAT

"Do you have any idea why the car left the highway?" continued Wade.

"No. I was in a daze. Maybe he went to sleep. But I keep thinking something bumped the back of our car. Like another vehicle nudged us. But I didn't see headlights or taillights on the road as we dived into the water."

Wade frowned thoughtfully. After a few minutes, he asked, "Do you remember anything else?"

"No." replied Doris. "Well, yes. As I woke up realizing we were about to wreck, Craig said something like, 'I was afraid this might happen.'"

"What did that mean?" asked Wade.

"I dunno. I thought we might have bad tires on the car, and Craig was apprehensive one might fail."

Changing the subject, Wade asked Doris, "How well did Craig like being the bank manager?"

"Great!" said Doris. "He was so eager to go to work each day. He liked the employees and his customers. He even worked late at night several times a month."

"How late?"

"Oh, he had to work late on Fridays because that was payday for most of his customers. They needed to deposit their checks and maybe get some cash. Other times he would stay there until midnight or after. Something about paperwork required by the Federal Reserve. I would already be asleep bed when he came home," Doris added, while trying to gain her composure.

"Also, a couple of Saturdays or Sundays a month. Not for long, but our time together would be interrupted. He would always come back in a good mood. Later Craig would make up our lost time together by taking me to a cozy restaurant where he would surprise me with a gift!"

"What kind of gift?" asked Sally.

"Oh, nice ones, like diamond earrings or gold jewelry. One time, a three carat diamond ring." She held up her hand, showing the ring as she explained. "I thought those presents were too expensive for him to afford on his salary. He said they were paid for from the rent off his family farm at Lodi that a Mr. Wilson works."

"That makes sense," replied Sally.

"I don't keep up with farming. I didn't know forty acres of soybeans could be so lucrative," admitted Doris.

CHAPTER 14
LARRY

Cade County had five lawyers practicing within its lines. Baxter had two; Central City three. Archie Baker was the youngest.

Archie was a sandy-haired, slender man, about six feet tall. He had grown up in Biloxi. His interests were few, but complex. He shot snooker, worked the daily crossword puzzle, played in euchre tournaments, and read classic literature. He loved baseball and was a devoted New York Yankee fan. He was a tee-totaler, but did drink Dr. Gilicuddy's Peppermint Schnapps on special occasions. His wife was a successful artist. She worked in a studio attached to their two-story Tudor house which was located in the oldest part of town. On weekends, she traveled to Chicago, Miami, and other large cities to sell her paintings. Archie and Tena had been in Central City for eleven years.

He had become financially independent the past year by successfully representing a devisee of the late Joab McMath in a will contest. Instead of retiring or hitting the bottle as many lesser attorneys would have, Archie became more determined to pursue his practice, to the dismay of many in his legal circles.

Generally, his courtroom behavior was obnoxious. Archie berated witnesses and was intentionally rude to judges and court clerks. However, he was a brilliant lawyer, probably because he had few hobbies and would relentlessly research and prepare his cases late at night and on weekends.

After his success defending the McMath will contest, new business poured into his office. Most of it was routine. He cherry-picked the cases, taking those that presented a legal challenge or those that could have a large settlement. He had mentioned around the Cade County Courthouse that he might have to take on an experienced associate.

Sheriff Powers was headed home for lunch on Friday. His route took him by Archie Baker's office which was located just off the town square in Central City. Archie had bought an older wood frame house which he had remodeled, at a minimum cost, to accommodate the needs of a law practice.

There was parking space in front of the building for clients. Archie and his staff parked in the rear.

As the building came into Grady's view, his jaw dropped and he exclaimed, "Holy smokes!" A battered, faded red 1958 Edsel convertible was parked squarely in front of the entrance. The rear of the car was covered in dust. Grady knew who owned this car. There was probably not another one of these in the whole country that was operable. It belonged to "Loophole" Larry Lawrence who had practiced law in Central City many years ago.

Larry had been a genius at researching the law, which he dearly loved. His early practice in Central City had suffered because he was always tending to his clients' affairs at the last minute. This tardiness was caused by his obsession with research. He was prompt with the necessary research of a client's case, but in the process, he would stumble across other cases that interested him. These cases had nothing to do with his client's issue, but he would read them, which led to other cases on other subjects. Larry would read and read. And read. This reading took time away from the remainder of his clients' needs, thus causing him to dangerously push deadlines.

One day he stumbled across a simple, but odd, case. And it had originated in Cade County. Otto, a now-deceased lawyer from Baxter, had sued a bank in town for mishandling his money. He asserted that the bank was deliberately posting his deposits into his savings accounts several days late. The lawyer's claim was that he lost earned interest.

The case went to trial. The bank's expert witness testified that the claim was bogus. She said that it was to the bank's favor to timely deposit Mr. Otto's money, for their profit on the average float of his funds far exceeded the amount of interest they would pay on the corresponding sum. "Anyway," she said, "even if this court ruled for Mr. Otto, he would only have earned an extra $19.17!" The judge ruled in the bank's favor.

Nonplussed, Otto appealed. Prudently, he represented himself so there would be no legal fees. Months later the Mississippi Supreme Court upheld the lower court's decision in part. The Court awarded Otto the $19.17 but disallowed his request for punitive damages.

For months, frugal Otto was the daily joke at the coffee shop. First, because of his efforts to recover $19.17; second, because he owned stock in the bank that he sued!

Larry had chuckled when he read the case. Otto was a drinking buddy of his, and they also rode together to Oxford for Ole Miss home football games each year. But the facts intrigued him. Especially, saving accounts and how they earned interest.

One of the excerpts of the expert's testimony had caught his eye. On the witness stand, she had explained how the bank calculated the amount of a customer's earned interest. She had stated, "At the end of the month, we deposit the calculated amount, after rounding up, into the customer's account."

Loophole wasn't that good with figures, and his law practice had never been involved with rates of interest. He thought interest earned on money was supposed to be calculated on shorter periods than monthly. Maybe compounded daily? He wondered if the banking industry was involved in some kind of financial scheme involving customers' savings accounts.

Since this occurred before technology had advanced enough to be commonplace, Larry traveled to the downtown Memphis public library. This library had a trove of business periodicals. He was able to compile an estimate of how many savings accounts existed in the country, along with the average total deposits.

The next week he leaned on a local CPA, Scotty Ames, for input. Scotty had a reputation of being eccentric. He did come across that way, but it was because he was extremely brilliant. He was also a genius with math.

Larry dropped by Scotty's office one morning. Tax season was in full swing, and Scotty was irritated because another professional had just dropped by without an appointment. But when Larry remarked that he was on to something that could be lucrative and that he would share with Scotty, the CPA's mood improved. "Come back into my personal office!" invited Scotty.

Larry took a chair. Scotty seated himself behind his desk and propped his feet onto his desk, rubber boots and all. He had run late that morning from feeding his cows at the barn on his nearby farm. Larry noticed that one boot was red and one was black, both having remnants of barnyard mud on the soles. Larry wrinkled his nose and scooted his chair further from the desk. Scotty didn't seem to mind the rancid atmosphere.

As Larry explained his scheme in detail, Scotty's eyes glazed. He told his secretary to cancel his appointments for the remainder of the morning. His rate of breathing increased when Larry said he would split his share of any recovery with Scotty.

"This will take a lot of manual work using my calculator, and we will need to find a tattletale in a bank somewhere to verify what may be going on," said Scotty.

"I have a former classmate who grew up in Baxter and who now works in the computer section of a big bank in St. Louis. He owes me a favor. I'll give him a call."

"What kind of favor does he owe you?" wondered Scotty.

Larry explained. "A bunch of us were coming back to the Ole Miss campus from a party at Sardis Lake one night. Doug was driving, and he and everybody else in the car except me was drunk. I would have been too, had I not been taking some high-powered allergy medicine and had to refrain. Anyway, I was on the front seat. All of a sudden, blue lights appeared behind us. Doug panicked, but I coaxed him into switching positions. We were able to do that quickly and without causing the car to weave before we were stopped."

"Sounds like you had done that before," smirked Scotty.

"Yup! Doug was forever grateful."

Larry made the call to his friend, who assured him that he could snoop without anyone knowing.

A week later, Doug called back. He was speaking urgently in a low voice, "Man, you are on to something! I'm shocked at what I found! Now, you have to cut me in on this!"

"What did you find?"

"At the end of each day, the interest earned by the owner of each savings account is calculated. The amount is reduced to three decimal places, but the customer only gets the benefit of the second decimal. For example, if the amount calculated is $.423, forty-two cents is deposited into the customer's account."

"What happens to the third number?" puzzled Larry.

"This may be where you can hit a home-run," said the friend. "The bank is not ignoring this fraction. They are sliding the amount, which could be from $.001 to $.009, into a secret account, knowing that no customer would ever notice."

"Wow!" exclaimed Larry.

"Yeah! That's not much, but when you have a large number of accounts, the amount can add up. I sneaked around and found that my bank siphoned off $75,000 last year from this maneuver."

Doug added, "Don't forget me at Christmas!"

Larry laughed.

Larry passed the information on to Scotty. In a few days, Scotty came up with a rough estimate of how much a nationwide manipulation of interest could total.

Larry got busy and contacted a law firm in Jackson, Mississippi, that had branches in other large cities. The firm filed a class-action suit against all major banks in the nation. The case attracted media attention, and its progress was mentioned weekly by the national news networks.

Eventually, the plaintiffs prevailed with a multi-million-dollar judgment along with an even greater punitive damage award. The defendants appealed. In lieu of a required expensive appeal bond, the court allowed a waiver if the money awarded, including the attorneys' fees, was immediately placed in escrow with a reputable national clearinghouse.

The amount of the legal fees from the judgment was staggering! Larry became a multi-millionaire on paper at the age of twenty-eight. He was a guest on most of the daily talk shows. He was tagged with the nickname "Loophole," for no other lawyer had ever contemplated his idea.

While the case was on appeal, the principals of the clearing house, without authority, began to use the money they were holding to speculate on the world currency markets, thinking their investment was a "sure-thing." However, the economies of several third-world countries went south, causing the financial markets to become negatively volatile. The entire investment was lost.

The clearinghouse filed for bankruptcy. Fortunately, Larry had not spent money that he didn't have.

But Scotty had. Anticipating the arrival of his windfall in the not-too-soon future, Scotty put every penny he had into soybean futures contracts. He had been a shrewd trader for a few years and knew the markets well enough to identify profitable movements. As soybean prices slowly moved upward, he would buy as many contracts on a 10% margin as his paper profits would allow. Eventually, he had built a pyramid. When Scotty got the news that his expected lawsuit fee had vanished, soybeans prices were also falling. He had to liquidate his positions, for now he had no money to cover his margins. In the end, Scotty managed to break even, but he blamed Larry for his loss of phantom profits.

Larry fell into a deep depression and began to drink. He lost interest in his law practice. He didn't show up at the office most days, especially if the weather was nice. His lifestyle became similar to that of a hippy, and he was also having to dodge his friend Scotty who scolded him at every opportunity and also billed him each month for the amount of the lost fees.

Finally, he came to his senses and searching for work, traveled to the Gulf Coast in the old Edsel he had taken as a legal fee defending a client on a burglary charge. He was hired by a local district attorney's office to prosecute criminals, which was opposite of his love of representing defendants.

Some of his friends even went to the trouble of writing a letter which ridiculed him for changing sides in the criminal justice system. The letter was loaded with humor and dragged in past sins of other lawyers. The essay was favorably greeted as it circulated within the area's legal circles.

Larry would travel to Central City a few times a year to visit his sister and to hang out with old friends. But for the most part, he had become semi-forgotten.

The sheriff reflected, "I hope this is only a visit. Surely Archie is not taking ole Larry into his practice!"

CHAPTER 15
MOLLIE'S REWARD

As Wade pulled into the sheriff's office at noon, he noticed an older car with a dented fender parked in the visitor's slot. It looked familiar. When he entered the building, he saw a frail, young lady in a worn dress sitting at the end of the sofa in the lounge. She was twisting her hands anxiously. Her tatty purse was beside her. A cereal box was next to her feet.

He recognized Mollie Carver, for he had attended the auction when her late husband's farm equipment had been sold shortly after his death. She spoke, "Mr. Hampton, can I see you for a minute? I'm on my lunch hour, and I won't be long."

Wade nodded, "Sure, Mrs. Carver. Come into my office."

Mollie placed the box on his desk. Nervously, she said, "I'm scared. I need to show you something."

She turned the box of Lucky Charms upside down and poured bundles of money onto the desk. Wade stared! There were many rolls of used bills, and each roll was bound by a rubber band. He opened one and counted the money. She stood nervously as he counted. Then Wade calculated the total by multiplying the number of rolls. He estimated that the box held $80,000!

He raised his eyebrows and asked, "Where did this come from?"

Mollie took a seat on the edge of the nearest wooden chair and explained how it came into her possession. Wade asked, "Who knows about this?"

"No one," said Mollie. "Gracie promised she wouldn't tell anyone. And Harry is too young to understand. What should I do?" she continued.

"Leave it here in our custody. I'll do an investigation and see if I can find the owner."

"Thank you," said Mollie. "I've been so worried. I don't want to get into trouble." She got up to leave.

Wade called to her as she was passing through the door, "Wait a minute."

He opened his desk drawer and pulled out a thousand dollars of his own money. "Here, take this. There is always a reward paid when lost money is found," he fibbed.

Mollie protested, "Oh, Mr. Hampton, I can't take that. The money doesn't belong to me."

Wade persisted firmly, "Take it. If the owner offers more, I'll see that you get it."

Mollie sobbed as he placed the bills into her hand. She tightly hugged him. "Thank you! We need this so much!"

A few minutes after she left, the sheriff arrived. He saw the empty cereal box and the money on Wade's desk. Wade had opened all the bundles and stacked the bills.

"Where did that come from?" the sheriff asked.

Wade told him Mollie's story and said, "More found money! The box held $87,300!"

"I think this is different from what's been found around the county so far."

Wade agreed, "These are all old twenties. The others were all new hundreds."

"A fresh mystery," Grady commented thoughtfully. "Just what we need. Go over to that store in Vena and see what you can discover."

That afternoon, Wade drove over to the Farm-to-Fork in Vena. He found the owner, Rydell Keeton, in the condiment aisle arranging catsup bottles on a shelf. They spoke. Wade joked, "I thought you would be retired by now."

Rydell gave him a firm stare and said, "I've got five reasons why not. And they are all in college."

Wade laughed. Then he told Rydell about Gracie finding the Lucky Charms box filled with money in his Poor Box a couple of nights ago. "Is that where you keep your cash?"

Rydell was puzzled. "That's not my money. I have no idea where it came from."

He thought for a while and said, "That's the day we filled the Poor Box. My high school stocker is in the back right now. Come on. We'll talk to him."

Wade cautioned, "Don't tell him about the money."

"You got that right," agreed Rydell. "If word got around that money is stuffed in boxes in my store, my shelves will get trashed."

Rydell found the stocker and asked, "Do you remember a box of Lucky Charms being in the Poor Box on Tuesday?"

"Oh, sure. I put it there when I filled the box," said the boy.

"Was it in the cart of bargain items that had been collected over the weekend?" asked Rydell.

"No. I brought it from the storeroom. It was by itself in the bin of dog food that was delivered earlier."

"Bin of dog food? What was the cereal doing in there?" asked Rydell.

"I dunno," said the boy. "I thought that was odd. It was squeezed against the side of the bin toward the bottom."

DRIVER'S FLAT

Wade and Rydell walked to the store front.

"Where does the dog food come from?" asked Wade.

"Usually from the factory at Louisville. The truck drops off feed at a few stops before it gets here," said Rydell.

As he left the store, Wade asked Rydell to inquire of the driver on his next delivery if he knew how the cereal box got into his truck.

CHAPTER 16
CLYTEE

It was hump day, and Lola's was crowded at lunch time. The community table was full, as were most of the booths and the tables in the rear. Clytee Lott, a striking, gray-haired widow, was seated by herself in the front booth and was facing the entrance.

Her father had become immensely wealthy by acquiring forest lands in the area during the depression and selling the cypress timber to the Navy during WWII. The cypress was used to make landing crafts. Clytee was an only child and inherited the family fortune. Today, she was wearing her short fur coat and an expensive pearl necklace; her make-up was immaculate. Clytee had a reputation of speaking her thoughts while using risqué language to the dismay of her friends. She reveled in telling off-color jokes, some of which were on herself. Her language, though never vulgar, could cause some listeners to be uncomfortable.

Clytee had many friends and never missed a social gathering, which was always lively with her in attendance. She didn't drink to excess at the parties although she nipped on a Jim Beam bottle nightly. A few years ago, her granddaughter, who was a flight attendant with Delta, suggested that she write a social column for *The Whisperer,* a weekly newspaper in Cade County. The granddaughter thought it would make the paper more entertaining and would give Clytee an excuse to mix and mingle more often.

Clytee jumped on the idea and coaxed Winslow Percy, the editor of the paper, to include her article. At first, he was reluctant, but after Clytee pointed out his paper didn't really offer female readers any social news, he agreed. He told her he would run the column on a trial basis for a few weeks. They had argued about a name for the column. Clytee prevailed, and the column was known as "Clytee's Problem Page."

She led off her column by printing a question from a female reader which could be about a personal problem, where to find a certain recipe, how to make plumbing repairs, a social issue, a health problem, and such. Or it could just be about current news. Clytee would furnish the answer in appropriate detail. Then came the interesting part. She would add her own thoughts, which usually descended into gossip and innuendos about unnamed persons. She was skillful in moving her readers away from a mundane question into a wild diatribe.

Her responses prompted her readers to begin to send in salacious questions, which caused her article to be the most interesting one in the paper.

The first column handled a question from someone named "Kate." Without identifying the persons, Kate wrote that a certain man had recently lost his wife to cancer, and within two months, he had married a much younger woman.

Her question was, "Wasn't that a little too soon, and wasn't something already going on?"

Clytee replied, "Oh, no. I was at the funeral. The romance got started right there when their eyes met across the casket!"

Social media went wild with speculation of who Kate and the newlyweds were. Few believed Clytee's reply. The column was an instant success.

Clytee's second column increased readership. This time the letter was from "Emma" who stated that she had attended a Black Friday Sale at a women's clothing store in Memphis the previous Thanksgiving. The store's aisles were filled with tables piled high with merchandise. A mob of females had formed outside the store. When the doors were opened, the shoppers streamed by both sides of the tables, wildly sorting through the items. Emma claimed that she saw a certain woman who worked in the courthouse at Poston reach across a table and gleefully snatch a silk scarf out of another shopper's hands. Her question was, "Shouldn't she be fired?"

Clytee, with the goal of making her column the centerpiece of the paper, replied, "That question should be answered by my readers. I'll print the ten most popular answers in next week's edition at the end of my column." This response caused her readers to become busy trying to discover who all worked at the courthouse in order to lay the blame on the most likely candidate.

The third letter caught the most attention from the older women in the county. It was from an unnamed female who claimed she was a member of the national Anti-Saloon League. It narrated that two certain ladies were regular shoppers in a nearby town that was wet, but only hot beer was allowed to be sold. The ladies would travel there each week to buy a long list of groceries. Upon entering the market, they would get a six-pack of hot beer and hide it in the frozen-food lockers. Thirty minutes later as they headed to the checkout with full carts, they would retrieve the cold beer to enjoy on the drive home. The clerks never noticed.

The question to Clytee was, "Shouldn't someone tell that store what's going on? I know who they are and both of them sit on the front row of the church."

Her reply was, "Let the pews speak for themselves!"

Needless to say, the front pews in all of the county Baptist churches were vacant the next Sunday.

Clytee had ordered her meal and was sipping coffee when the door abruptly swung open. The customer took one step inside and stopped, looking the crowded dining area over. He was the newly hired band director at the high school. Ron had moved to Central City from Rolling Fork and was still a stranger to most. His appearance reflected a state of irritability. Clytee recognized Ron's dilemma: whether or not there was room for one more diner. Since she was the only one in her booth, Clytee was willing for him to join her. She spoke, "Young man, are you looking for a seat?"

He looked down at this woman, whom he didn't know, and snarled, "I have a seat. I'm looking for a place to put it!"

Clytee, who had never taken bull from anyone, responded quickly, "Well, son, it has a hole in it. Why don't you hang it on the hat rack over there in the corner?"

The guys at the community table roared, and the diners in the back, who had also overheard, joined in, some slapping their tables.

Ron's face turned bright red, and his departure was more abrupt than his arrival. Several patrons chimed in, "Lay it to him, Clytee." One said, "He'll be dodging you!" "Put that in your column," suggested another.

Deputy Wade Sumrall, who had finished his meal at the counter, eased into the booth across from her. He laughed, "I heard that! You ole smart alec!"

Clytee giggled. She adored Wade. His steely eyes reminded her of her late husband's.

Wade asked, "Clytee. I've known you for a long time, and I need a favor."

She reached across the table and held Wade's gnarled hand wrapped around his coffee mug and said coyly, "Why, of course. I would love to hold a debt on you!"

Wade blushed helplessly, for Clytee's charm was irresistible.

He spoke, "In your last column you hinted that you had a source that could explain where all that money that's being found is coming from. I need to interview that person."

"Now, Wade, since I'm now writing a column in the paper, I have become a journalist. You being a lawman, and a good one at that, I might add, should know I don't have to reveal my sources."

Wade cleared his throat. "As a personal favor?"

"No. I can't do that. I might need my source again."

"Okay," replied Wade.

Clytee said, "I take it your investigation has hit a brick wall?"

"Yup. We have several ideas about the source. We're chasing them down. We just need more time."

"I will help you on that. I'll string out some hints in my future columns. That'll keep my readers coming back."

"Well, thanks," said Wade, as he got up to leave.

Clytee looked at him with a twinkle in her eyes and confided, "Sometimes you can find the treasure you seek in a junkyard."

Wade stared at her for a second and blurted, "Why, you sly ole dog!" He made a mental to forward the tip to the sheriff.

Clytee tittered as she watched Wade go out the door.

Wade went back to his office and told the sheriff about his conversation with Clytee.

Grady snorted. "That doesn't surprise me at all. She is playing her readers. She knows what interests them. I've been suspecting her of making up the stuff that she adds to her column."

Wade grinned. "Yeah! She is a shrewd woman. She has them believing some of the rubbish she writes!"

Grady admitted, "You can put me on that list, too. My wife scolds me for reading her column." Grady's wife had taught English and literature at Central City High for many years, and the column irritated her because of the way Clytee consistently botched the grammar.

"She did assure me that if she received any correspondence that alluded to a confession about the money source, she would give me a call."

Grady responded, "That's good. I've a feeling that whoever is throwing the money around will eventually want credit."

DRIVER'S FLAT

CHAPTER 17
SHIFTY

Wade had called Fred, the FBI agent in Oxford, to report the cereal box cash. He relayed his concerns that this money could be contraband. Fred became interested and said he would drive down to Poston and meet with the sheriff's staff.

The meeting was interrupted by a clamor in the parking lot. Fred walked to the window and stared out. The racket continued and became even louder.

Fred announced without turning his head, "This is the first time I've seen an Irish potato in a yellow jumpsuit!"

The others moved to the window. Outside was a Mississippi Highway Patrolman wrestling a stocky man out of his squad car. The state trooper had his hands full! The man was heavy-set. His head just barely stuck out from his shoulders because his neck was so short. Several large warts were visible on his neck and head. His hair was closely cropped; his skin was red. The man's body was broad, and he was dressed in a yellow jumpsuit and cowboy boots.

Fred asked, "Who in the world is that?"

Wade chuckled. "That's Shifty McCord. He's one of our local characters. He owns a large block of land in the south end of the county and raises cows and soybeans. Sometimes cotton."

The sheriff mused, "And that's Joe Dubuisson, our new, young state trooper from the Gulf Coast. I think he is about to learn that sometimes it's best just to let well enough alone."

In a few minutes, the state trooper entered the room. He was breathing heavily. "Man," he said, "that guy gave me a tussle on that arrest."

"What was that all about?" asked Wade.

"He made an illegal turn under the traffic light at the feed-store in Baxter. I pulled him over and discovered that his license had expired, his tag had expired, and his inspection sticker had expired. I was going to give him a ticket, but he proceeded to tell me how important he was and who all he knew in the state capital. When I told him all that wasn't going to help, he gave me a good cussin'!"

"So?" asked Wade.

"He refused to get out of his car. I dragged him out, and he began to wrestle me. I thought I was strong, but that man was like a bull. He finally gave out, so I was able to subdue him. I just got him booked."

"Sammy, go down and make sure Shifty is okay."

Deputy Baker left and came back shortly. "He's just skinned up. But he wants us to call his family to go get his old car at the feed store. Shifty said he had a bunch of dog food in there that somebody might steal."

Wade nodded.

Sammy said, "Every time I meet him in the road he has the back seat and the floorboard of that old car filled with dog food sacks."

"Yeah. He has been raising hunting dogs out on his farm the last few years. He sells them across the country," replied Wade.

"His dogs are eatin' pretty good," noted Deputy Sammy.

FBI agent Fred was intrigued with the cereal box and its contents. He carefully examined the bills and then blurted, "This is drug money! I know because I've seen too much of this."

"That's what we concluded," replied Sheriff Powers.

"I'll take some of the rolls back and let Swanson, our drug dog, give them a sniff."

"Give us a report."

As Fred took a roll from the box, he halted and stared.

Wade noticed and asked, "What's wrong?"

Fred didn't answer. He flipped his phone open to his photos and scrolled. He stopped at one which he enlarged. "Look at this," he ordered.

The others looked over his shoulder at a picture of an assortment of trash on a floor. Fred said, "This was taken at the bank in Driver's Flat after the robbery. It's the floor of the vault."

They could see broken drill bits, scattered lockbox drawers, a blue baby shoe, photographs, pieces of silverware, letters, and scraps of paper.

Fred commented, "Look at that piece of red paper by the door of the vault closet."

The torn scrap was small and had a yellow "y" near what appeared to be a horse's nose.

Fred placed his camera screen near the front of the Lucky Charms box on the table.

Sally Ryder, the deputy, exclaimed, "Hell! I mean heck. That's a match."

"What in the world would a box of Lucky Charms be doing in a bank vault?" asked Wade. "They're not that valuable."

The room was silent as they all absorbed this evidence and contemplated whether or not the two boxes, ninety miles apart, were connected.

Fred observed, "The cereal box wasn't in a lockbox because it wouldn't fit into even the largest one in this bank."

Finally, as Fred stuffed the sample currency into his case and headed for the door, Sally snickered after him, "Fred, you now have the 'Cereal Box Bandits' in your bailiwick!"

CHAPTER 18
POLITICS

Sheriff Grady Powers was sitting in his recliner at home watching the local evening news and trying to relax. The day had been long and difficult: a wreck fatality; several domestic disputes; and a hunt for a lost person.

The phone rang just as the weather lady was beginning to describe a tornado threat. The caller was the circuit clerk. "I'm sorry to bother you at home, but I have some good news and some bad news," he said.

Grady groaned inwardly, "Now what?" He gruffly commanded, "Well, give me the bad news first."

"Today was the last day for candidates to qualify to run for county office. Until 4:55 p.m., all of us elected officials had no opposition." A small silence. Then he continued, "Except one."

"Oh?" asked Grady worriedly.

"Yes, you."

"Who is my opposition?"

"Shifty McCord!"

"Oh, my word! Of all people!"

"Well, the good news is you won't have a problem being re-elected. You've been sheriff for two terms already, and everybody likes you and the good job you've done."

"Well, thanks," replied Grady.

DRIVER'S FLAT

The clerk's remarks of assurance bounced off Grady. He recalled the advice of the late Mr. Moore, a distinguished lawyer in Central City, who had a wise-crack about political candidates: "Any time an incumbent has opposition, even of a token nature, he has to assume that he has lost forty percent of the votes on the day the opponent announces."

Grady asked the clerk, "Any background on why Shifty is running?"

"No. He made bond today on all those traffic charges. He made a beeline to my office with his qualifying papers. Apparently, he already had those at the time he got arrested. Shifty blew off steam about how it was time Cade County made some progress and changes. He said the last few days behind bars qualified him to run a jail properly. He said he knew most of the criminals in the county and that you had no idea of what was going on under your nose."

"Sounds like his usual hot air," said Grady.

"He did make one strange remark."

"What?"

"Shifty said if he was elected sheriff, he would make the county go green."

DRIVER'S FLAT

PART TWO

A FLASHBACK TO THE PREVIOUS YEAR

DRIVER'S FLAT

DRIVER'S FLAT

CHAPTER 19
THE HITCHHIKER

Over six months ago and one hundred miles away, an unusual accident occurred which would connect to, and eventually overshadow, the Cade County money mystery.

On the north side of I-55 in West Memphis, Arkansas, a slender hitchhiker was thumbing a ride. He had just walked from Memphis across the bridge that spanned the Mississippi River. He was a seventy-six-year-old man with well-groomed gray hair. He was wearing gray slacks, a white shirt with an open collar, a navy blazer, and a candy-striped skimmer hat. At his feet was a leather shoulder bag, which contained several changes of clothes, his shaving gear, and a variety of personal items. An expensive mandolin leaned against the bag.

The early September day was nice. The sun was shining and the weather was warm. Marvin had been standing there for a while without catching a ride. He decided to cross the lanes to try his luck in the other direction. He was a professional traveler and had crisscrossed the country often. Marvin had time on his hands, so it didn't matter in which direction his travels would carry him.

He safely traversed the traffic in all lanes and set his bag and mandolin on the shoulder. Then he noticed a tear in the bottom of the paper sack he held in his hand. He looked back and saw a bundle of crackers and a can of Vienna sausages on the center line of the traffic lane. Marvin hastened to grab the food before it got squashed. As he turned back, he stumbled and fell to a knee.

The driver of an oncoming delivery truck loaded with oxygen bottles, glanced down at his cell phone and panicked when he looked up and saw the hitchhiker in his lane. The driver prematurely swerved into the back end of an 18-wheeler that was passing him. The impact caused the delivery truck to overturn on its side and skid down the pavement. A green cylinder left the truck's bed, tumbled end-over-end a couple of times, became airborne, and finally sailed crossways into the chest of Marvin, who had regained the safety of the shoulder. The clout knocked him into the ditch.

Closely following the oxygen truck was a new, 3-axle rotator tow truck driven by its owner, Rickey, who had a wrecker business outside of Central City. Close behind the rotator was Rickey's cousin, Tony, who was driving a cargo truck, returning to Cade County from St. Louis. Fifty-year-old Tony had been driving trucks since age fourteen, when his grandpa started sending him to Tennessee to haul gravel. Grandpa had modified the truck seat so Tony could see out of the cab.

The day before, he had carried a load of dog food from the factory in Louisville, Mississippi, to St. Louis, and Rickey rode with him to pick up the rotator from a custom paint shop. The black and purple paint job portrayed a huge Viking scene of semi-clad, pretty young women wearing animal skins with swords in their hands. The unique design had been an eye-catcher all the way down the interstate. The two drivers had put their pedals to the metal the entire trip.

Both drivers were caught by surprise by the instant crash in front of them. With the driver reacting hurriedly, the rotator swerved to the left of the wreck. Because Tony had been on

DRIVER'S FLAT

the rotator's rear bumper, he had even less time to react. His driving experience enabled him to take the shoulder on the right and jockey his vehicle through a flying melee of dust, papers, and trash to safely clear the wreckage. Neither saw the body in the ditch. Nor did Tony's sleeping passenger who had caught a ride with him in St. Louis.

Looking in their rear-view mirrors and thinking there was nothing they could do to help, the drivers continued onward to Cade County without slowing.

An Arkansas trooper arrived on the scene. He got statements from the drivers of the 18-wheeler and delivery truck plus the two occupants of a pickup who had stopped on the adjacent frontage road to get drinks from the cargo bed of their truck. These field hands had witnessed the accident.

Since the wreck had occurred within sight of the Harahan Bridge over the Mississippi River, the trooper called the Last Journey Funeral Home in Memphis to transport the body. The trooper sniggered to himself, "That's just another homeless bum, and I'll let the taxpayers in Memphis foot all costs!" He figured his supervisor would approve that call with glee. He might even get a couple of extra days off in the upcoming deer season and probably a free weekend in the funeral home owner's condo in Destin.

The undertaker at the Last Journey Funeral Home and his assistant processed the body. They searched through his wallet for an identity. A card contained information that the deceased was Marvin Fant; it also had the name of a contact person with a telephone number. A call to the number revealed that the contact was a friend who lived in Cade County, Mississippi. The undertaker thought the friend sounded like an older,

DRIVER'S FLAT

uneducated redneck. He gave the name of a funeral home in a nearby county that would haul the body for burial. The friend assured him that Marvin's family had the means to pay their expenses.

The undertaker, after instructing Ned to inventory the contents of the leather bag, left the room. The assistant wearily sorted through clothes, an assortment of medicines (none being narcotics), a couple of used bus tickets, a receipt from a boarding house in Wheeling, West Virginia, and a recent ticket from a Cardinals home baseball game. His interest peaked when he found $2,000 inside a sock. Being behind in child support, he slipped $1,900 into his pocket and inventoried one bill. He next found a diamond and gold Omega watch with a broken leather band inside a box. The box went into the pocket with the bills. This was not his first rodeo.

He justified the take as a fringe benefit due him for the low salary his boss paid and the unpleasant working conditions he was exposed to from time to time. He omitted the mandolin from the inventory list.

CHAPTER 20
THE PAWNBROKER

The next day, Ned, the assistant undertaker, visited Comfort and Trust, one of the oldest pawn shops in Memphis. It was located on Poplar just east of downtown. Ned opened the metal door and passed under the customary three orange spheres suspended above. He was a regular. The owner, Leduc Bassange, motioned him to his back office away from a scattering of customers. Leduc was a small, swarthy Frenchman in his late seventies. He was wearing a black beret and was puffing away on a bent Butz-Choquin pipe clenched in his jaw. His great-grandfather had founded the business upon his arrival in America around 1900. Leduc was now the sole proprietor. His name was also listed in certain black books as a high-end recéleur. Ned's visits were infrequent, but always lucrative for Leduc.

"What is it this time?" Leduc asked. He suspected, but didn't want to know, the source of Ned's pledges. He always carried the transactions with Ned as a loan, rather than a purchase, knowing that the hocked items wouldn't be reclaimed.

Ned pulled the box from his briefcase and handed it to Leduc. The watch was thoroughly examined by Leduc. He confirmed that the case was 18K gold. The brand was also good for resale. Leduc then made an offer which startled Ned. He didn't really know watches but had not expected this one to be worth so much. Without thinking, Ned blurted, "That's a top watch for a hitchhiker to own!"

Leduc looked him over and raised an eyebrow, "Oh?"

Ned stammered, "Forget it. It's nothing."

Leduc asked, "You did say it fell from a truck?"

"Yeah. Yeah. That's right!" Ned hastily confirmed.

He asked for more money, but Leduc wouldn't budge. A deal was made, and when the money was in his hands, Ned stated, "I may be able to deliver a nice mandolin later."

At the end of the day after the shop was closed, Leduc tagged all pieces of merchandise that had been brought in. When he pulled the Omega watch from its box, he noticed what appeared to be a false bottom. He fetched a knife and pried up a felt-covered piece of cardboard. Underneath were some scraps of paper with names and locations of about ten banks with possible account numbers listed. The banks were scattered around the country: Shreveport, Birmingham, Miami, Wichita, Grand Junction, Kansas City, Red Lodge, Paragould, and one in Houston, Mississippi. Another scrap had three sets of numbers: a routing number of a bank accompanied by a double digit, which Leduc surmised were lockbox numbers. Underneath the paper scraps were several small, black-and-white photographs of what might be family members and one of a man seated at a table with an attractive woman who was playing with some kind of odd-looking toy. The photo seemed to be in a club, and the two wore broad smiles.

Leduc pulled out a magnifying glass and peered at the photograph. He noticed a matchbook, laying on the table's edge. He moved the picture closer and saw a name on the

DRIVER'S FLAT

cover: Crimson Feather. Leduc knew that to be a supper club with regular live entertainment on Brooks Road in South Memphis. Thoughtfully, Leduc placed the notes back into the watch box but left the photographs on top of the desk.

The next morning, Leduc called one of his regular buyers. Leduc had a list of patrons to whom he could pass expensive items off the record for a profit.

The Memphis police suspected Leduc of having contacts in Russian organized crime. The police had not linked the Russians to any activity in Memphis but knew they were active in New Orleans and St. Louis. Since Memphis was halfway between these cities, it would only be a matter of time until they appeared. Although Leduc, along with most pawnshop owners in town, was on the police radar, he had not been officially connected to these gangsters.

At five o'clock, Yuri Popov arrived. He was a tall, lanky man with a long nose and a black beard. Yuri was wearing black clothes and a black hat. His appearance caused him to come across as an Orthodox Jew. His speech carried a slight foreign accent. He greeted Leduc warmly and said they needed to get down to business. They went into the back office for privacy.

Yuri whistled when he was shown the watch, "Nice!"

"Yeah! That's one of the more expensive watches that Omega made. And it's old, " replied Leduc. "They quit making this line of watches years ago."

They dickered back and forth over the price and finally agreed on a number. Yuri pulled a bundle of bills from his attaché case, paid Leduc, and put the watch and its box into his case. Then they each downed a stiff shot of vodka to celebrate the trade.

As Yuri placed his empty glass on the desk, he spied the picture of the man and woman in the club. He picked it up and

DRIVER'S FLAT

studied it with interest. Finally, he asked, "Where did you get this?"

"It was in the bottom of the watch box," Leduc answered.

"Who owned the box?"

"I don't know," said Leduc. "But I think it came from a dead hitchhiker. There are some notes in the watch box, but they didn't have any information that would identify the owner."

"Can I keep this photograph?" asked Yuri.

"Sure. It goes with the watch, along with these other photographs."

Yuri kept looking at the club photograph.

Discreetly, Leduc noticed Yuri's eyes focus on the bottom of the picture.

"What is that object the woman has in her hands?" Leduc asked.

Yuri wasn't sure. "The room where the picture was made is sort of dark, and I can't tell."

"It looks like a child's toy," said Leduc. "When do you think the photo was made?"

"I dunno. It has to be old if you consider the style of clothes the people are wearing."

Yuri left the pawnshop and drove down to the bus station on Union Avenue. He pulled change from the box of quarters he kept on his floorboard and went to a payphone. He dialed a number in Germany and noted their local time as the phone was ringing. After midnight.

A groggy voice answered the call. Yuri was scolded for the late call, but then the interlocutor listened with interest to the message. He asked Yuri to scan and send the photograph. When Yuri explained that the quality of the picture was too poor to scan and transmit, the voice commanded sharply, "We need to meet!"

Yuri replied, "I'll fly over tomorrow."

Leduc was still at his desk gloating over his watch deal with Yuri. He leaned back in his chair and stared at the fly-specked, heart pine ceiling through the slowly turning blades of the ceiling fan. He wondered why Yuri wanted the photos. Did they have some kind of value? Was either of the persons in the club picture famous?

An uneasy feeling worked its way into his stomach causing him to wish Yuri hadn't seen the photos. But then he remembered that he had made copies of the pictures and the contents of the watch box. He had a friend who had been a regular in the Crimson Feather for years. Leduc decided that the friend should view the photographs.

CHAPTER 21
THE SEPTEMBER CLUB LUNCH

The telephone was ringing in Henry's house as he returned from collecting rent on some of his housing units. Out of breath, he picked the receiver up on its tenth ring. Thinking it would be a telemarketer, he gruffly answered, "Hello!" But it was an old friend in Memphis, Leduc Bassange.

"Been out jogging?" teased Leduc.

"You know me better than that, Leduc. That's a waste of time."

They visited briefly about some common friends. Then Leduc said, "I may be on to something. And I need your help."

"What about?" asked the Musician.

"I don't know. But someone I know is also interested, which gives me a feeling that a score may be in the works."

Ordinarily, the Musician would ridicule a revelation of this kind from anyone else. But, coming from Leduc, the statement was serious. He also knew that Leduc wouldn't reveal any more on the telephone.

Henry Childs replied, "I need to come to Memphis. Why don't we meet for lunch? The Crimson Feather?"

Leduc replied sharply, "No. The September Club. Tomorrow."

Henry agreed and hung up; his interest piqued. He had lived in Memphis off and on most of his life and had been a regular in the nightlife scene. The roughest clubs were in South Memphis with the September Club being the most unruly. Henry wondered why Leduc was choosing that location for lunch. It was a late-night, hard-core party place which didn't open until 9 p.m. But he knew that Leduc was tight with the owner, who had a reputation of obliging the requests of certain associates to have lunch or confidential meetings.

At one o'clock, Henry and Leduc were seated at a corner table near the stage of the September Club. They were the only diners. The staff was busy mopping the floor, positioning the tables, and preparing the bar for the night.

The waitress brought a dish of shrimp cocktail and a glass of unsweetened tea for Henry and an open-faced roast beef sandwich for Leduc with a cup of hot tea.

Henry asked, "Who's running your store?"

"My grandson. He's worked there enough that I can rely on him."

"Will he get the store when you retire?"

"More or less."

"When will that be?"

Leduc sniggered, "When they haul me out on a gurney."

"Yep. That's what I figured."

"What about you?" asked Leduc.

"As long as I can put a deal together, I'm gonna hang in there," replied Henry.

They became silent as they ate. Then Leduc leaned back from the table and said, "We've put a lot of deals together over the years, haven't we?"

DRIVER'S FLAT

Henry smiled, revealing his signature gold tooth. "We're the reason that alley in Central City got named Flimflam," he affirmed.

Leduc shoved his empty plate away, placed his pipe between his teeth, and relaxed as he puffed away. "Which deal did we do best on? The diamonds, the furs, or the TVs?"

Henry had lived with his grandmother on her farm outside Poston while in high school. Afterwards, he had briefly attended a local junior college and then moved to Memphis, which was only two hours away. He, like most of his buddies in high school, had worked for local farmers hauling hay and driving tractors. Henry had never held an eight-to-five job. After college, he had focused on jobs that paid commissions or involved selling or trading wares that generated a profit. For some years, his income had been touch-and-go. He wasn't satisfied; he liked nice things.

One day he had gone to Leduc's shop to pawn a watch belonging to his roommate, who worked as a deckhand on a towboat and wouldn't be back for six weeks. He and Leduc hit it off immediately. Leduc discovered that Henry hung around the kind of clientele that he needed. He offered Henry a cut of all the business he could send to the shop. This venture became profitable for both. Henry began to enjoy the role of a middleman.

Soon, Henry began to ask Leduc to allow him to take watches and jewelry out of the shop to sell. At first, Leduc was reluctant because he hadn't known the Musician that long and was afraid he might skip on him. To his amazement, Henry rarely returned with an unsold item. This went on for months. One day, Leduc asked, "How are you able to sell what you get from me? You're selling this stuff better than I can."

Henry replied, "I'll tell you if you'll cut me in on your bigger deals."

Leduc agreed.

Henry explained, "I take your stuff to Cade County, where I grew up. I know everybody there, so I call the ones I know will fall for a scam from the poolroom. I tell them to meet me in the alley outside the poolroom and not let the law see them. I park my car in the shadows and scoot down in the seat. When they get in the car, I make them scoot down. Then I show them the ring or watch, all the while looking in my rear-view with my ball cap pulled down low. By then, my mark is convinced the object is hot. I ask a jacked-up price and warn them not to be seen wearing it in Memphis. They fall for my pitch and buy the item every time!"

He rubbed his fingers together, smiled and said, "Ching! Ching!"

Henry smiled, "I'll vote for the TVs!"

Leduc said, "The atmosphere you had already established from your alley operations reeled in a ton of suckers on the TV deals."

Leduc had the "in" with a top executive at the headquarters of a local world-wide motel chain. The company would replace TV sets in their motels with newer models by the hundreds. Then they would dispose of the older ones however they could. They weren't concerned about getting the maximum price because the sets had already been written off their books. Leduc was able to buy the sets, to the exclusion of other customers, by passing a white envelope to the executive.

Henry said, "I would fill a rented pickup with sets, tarp them down, and park in the alley in Central City. I would go inside the poolroom and call my mark to meet me. I would flip the tarp up and only allow him a quick glance. I would be looking up and down the alley all the while. I would pitch that a friend had lifted them out of the motel company's warehouse. Never lost a sale."

Leduc laughed, "Well, you weren't lying. I did get them from the warehouse! At a near-nothing cost."

Leduc pulled the photocopies of the pictures from his jacket and said, "I want you to look at this picture taken in the Crimson Feather."

He then gave the Musician the story of how the picture came into his possession, along with the watch box. He showed Henry copies of its contents. "I sold the watch and its box to a discreet buyer, Yuri Popov. He asked questions about this picture and asked to keep it."

Henry's heart beat increased. He already knew Popov from a different direction. He knew that Leduc wasn't aware that he knew Popov, because Henry had never mentioned his name. If Popov had expressed interest in a random photograph, something was up. He would now have to be cautious with Leduc.

Leduc explained, "I'd like to know who those people are in that picture. The matchbook is from the Crimson Feather, which was your main hangout in Memphis. I thought you might recognize them."

Henry studied the picture. He figured it had been taken about thirty years ago. He knew the female, not as she appeared in the photograph, but as an older woman. He hadn't seen her in a while and didn't know where she was now. The man in the photo seemed familiar. Maybe someone he had seen on an irregular basis in the past?

In the picture, the man was obviously enjoying the company of the woman, who was extremely pretty. Both were smiling and posing. This club always had a photographer present to accommodate patrons who wanted a reminder of their nights out. The photographer made his money by selling his pictures at a premium.

Henry said, "The woman does look kinda familiar. Like someone who worked at the Crimson Feather when I first started hanging out there. Let me make some calls."

"Okay."

"Who did your friend seem most interested in, the man or the woman?"

"Neither. It was the toy the woman was holding," replied Leduc.

The remark caused Henry to take a second look at the picture, "What is that?"

"I have no idea," said Leduc.

On his way back to Cade County, Henry rethought his meeting with Leduc. The picture of the toy nagged at the back of his mind. Whatever it was, it was old. The lady seemed fascinated by it. Was it hers or his? Was it valuable?

He didn't let on to Leduc that he knew the woman. First, he needed to talk to her. That is, if she could be found.

Henry had always been an in-the-know individual. If he wasn't up on any subject, he always knew who was. He had a pawnshop contact in Las Vegas who might have an idea about the toy.

CHAPTER 22
THE HAT

The sun was high in the morning sky over Tony's house when he woke. He spun upright to the side of the bed, put his feet into wool slippers, and placed his elbows on his knees. With his head in his hands, he began to recount the events of his St. Louis trip. After they arrived there and unloaded Tony's cargo, he and Rickey had gone to the paint shop. It took them all night to help the workers finish installing the custom rigging on the rotator.

As they were about to leave the paint shop in St. Louis early the next morning, they received a call from a trucking buddy's wife in Central City. Her husband, Bobby Hubbard, was in the St. Louis city jail, and she asked them to get him out and bring him home. When asked why he was in jail, she snarled, "I don't know, and I don't want to know. He called me last night to come get him, but he was so drunk I couldn't understand his phony explanation."

On their way to the downtown jail in Tony's truck, Rickey said, "He's not riding with me. Knowing Bobby, he'll have one heck of a hangover. And I can't stand listening to him complaining for six hours. I'll kill him before we get home."

Tony replied, "Well, if Bobby's wife comes after him, she'll kill him! He can ride with me. But you'll owe me a big favor."

DRIVER'S FLAT

On the ride down the interstate, Tony quizzed Bobby about his arrest. Bobby explained that his truck had broken down on the outskirts of St. Louis. His company located a shop that would pull the rig in and repair it. Bobby was to catch a bus home, but the earliest trip south was the next day. He was dropped off at a shopping center where five motels were adjacent. He picked out an older one, checked into a room on the second floor, cleaned up, and headed to a nearby popular bar.

In the wee hours of the morning, he staggered back to his motel. He went up the metal stairs and around the corner to his room, which overlooked the swimming pool. He fiddled with the lock and became angry when the door wouldn't open. He went to the desk and had words with the clerk when she wouldn't give him a replacement key. He returned to his room, kicked the door and became loud and violent, waking the other guests. By the time he had wandered down to the pool in a rage and finished throwing all its furniture into the deep end, the police arrived. While arresting him, they explained that the reason the key wouldn't work was because he was at the wrong motel!

Tony ribbed Bobby about his predicament and how stupid-faced he had been. Bobby finally went to sleep with his head against the window.

Tony shaved, ate breakfast, and got into the cab of his truck to take it for service. As he pulled out of his drive, he noticed Bobby's wallet in the floorboard. He detoured to Bobby's house, pulled close to his bedroom window, and blew the truck's air horn until Bobby came outside.

Bobby was cussing him. Tony grinned, "Why are you so snarky, young man?"

"Because my head hurts. It feels like two bulldozers are in there, butting each other with their blades. And I'm in the doghouse!"

Then, facing the truck as he rubbed the sleep from his eyes, he observed, "You ain't too smart, yourself, using your grille for a hat rack."

"Huh?" puzzled Tony as he climbed down from the cab and walked to the front of the truck. There, between the grille and the radiator screen, was a colorful skimmer hat.

"Where did that come from?" wondered Tony as he pulled it off the screen.

Bobby replied, "Probably off the highway yesterday. You were bouncing your rig on and off the shoulder. Never had had such a rough ride. You stirred up all kinds of road trash."

Tony grinned. He had deliberately made the ride rough to worsen Bobby's hangover. He threw the hat into the cab and left Bobby's yard. The next day he went on a cross-country haul that would take a week to complete.

DRIVER'S FLAT

CHAPTER 23
MARVIN

At Lola's Coffee Shop, the regular crowd was at the community table, eager to partake in gossip. This morning, truth had again moved gossip to a back corner. Sensational news had arrived early. Marvin Fant had lost his life on the side of an interstate. Several versions of the accident were presented. Although there were variations in the stories, most told the facts.

Marvin had spent most of his life in Cade County and nearby Chickasaw County. A war veteran, he was known for his travels around the country as a hitchhiker. The only car he had ever owned was now an antique sitting on blocks in a storage building. Marvin was known by his jaunty dress, his handsome looks, and the mandolin that always accompanied him. He was a friendly fellow and attracted admirers. If a ride dropped him off in a town, he would wander toward the first visible group. Marvin would strike up a catchy, fast-moving tune and sing along. Invariably, the onlookers would pitch him money. He made enough at this to pay for his daily meals.

Several coffee drinkers gave accounts of his hitchhiking travels and how fast he moved around. One told about the time he watched Marvin try to catch a ride for an hour without success. He merely crossed the road and thumbed in the opposite direction. The crowd laughed at the notion that Marvin's lifestyle was such that it made no difference to him which way he traveled.

Another told about three local sailors, Wayne, Durwood, and Jim, who were stationed on the west coast some years back. They had a car out there, and when their ship docked in San Diego, they would head home for a thirty-day leave. They swore that on a return trip, Marvin was on the opposite side of the road at Greenwood thumbing a ride. The sailors drove straight through to California, one driving while the other two slept until their turn at the wheel was due. According to them, when they got to Arizona, Marvin was standing on their side of the highway with his thumb extended!

Then the conversation turned toward Marvin's reputation of being rich. These tales had abided for years. Rumors were that he owned a fancy restaurant in Los Angeles, a shopping center in Dallas, a charter boat in Destin, and a cattle ranch in Wyoming.

Little Ben Weaver, the local bird-dog trainer, recalled, "When I was a kid, Marvin ate supper one night with my uncle Harold. You know, Marvin grew up just down the road and was an old neighbor. While the family was eating, my cousin and I went through his leather bag. We found a receipt book where he was getting rent from a bunch of tenants in a building in New York City."

Mayor Todd West chimed in, "My nephew worked at First National Bank in Memphis one time. He had seen Marvin hitchhiking around here. One day he was in a crowd on the sidewalk at Third and Madison waiting for the light to change. He spied Marvin's hat ahead of him. My nephew decided he was going to follow Marvin to see what he was up to, even if it made him late getting to his desk. To his amazement, Marvin went into the bank. My nephew got on the elevator with

Marvin, who didn't know him, and was surprised to see that he got off on the bond floor. From the way he and the secretary greeted each other, it was obvious he was a regular. My nephew said Marvin had to have money if he was visiting this department."

Todd added, "And a few months later, coming back from lunch, my nephew saw Marvin walk off the street into the bank. He followed Marvin into the building and watched him go to the west side of the huge, three-story-high lobby and retrieve a paper bag from behind the curtains. He must have stashed the bag there while he went around town. Then Marvin walked down that long teller row on the first floor and smiled and waved at each pretty cashier. They all responded in kind as he went out the back."

Jon David Knox guffawed. "Yeah. One Saturday, he asked the owner of the Western Auto Store on the square if he could leave a sack of Viennas and crackers at the store while he shopped at other stores. Marvin let time slip by, and when he returned for his sack, Mr. Kimzey had locked up for the night. Marvin went to his house and made him go open the store so he could get his food! Mr. Kimzey gave him a stern talking-to about that!"

They all agreed that Marvin had been stingy enough to be rich. Little Ben remarked, "A friend over in Chickasaw County told me Marvin would regularly go to the soda fountain on the square in Houston at lunch and ask for a cup of hot water. He would pour catsup in the cup to make soup!"

DRIVER'S FLAT

CHAPTER 24
THE TIP

A call came in to Leduc from one of his snitches as he was about to lock the shop for the day. The guy was a driver for the only armored car service in Memphis. They served all the banks in the city and the nearby towns in a four-state area.

"I've picked up on something. Our deliveries to the bank in Driver's Flat just outside Memphis have recently increased. The amount of cash we pick up nearly matches," said the driver.

"How much is the increase?" asked Leduc.

"A lot. Until now, this stop was really for a minimum delivery because the bank is so small."

"What about the records on the cash you pick up?"

"They're in order."

"Notice anything unusual? Different people in charge of the bank? More customer activity?"

"Nope. But when we swing around the bank to leave, we pass the dumpster. It is always full on our delivery days. I guess we come by the day before the garbage is picked up. About the time our deliveries increased, my partner and I noticed the dumpster was always overflowing with empty, Lucky Charms cereal boxes. We figured someone is sneaking around the back and dumping their trash to hold their own garbage bill down."

Leduc was silent.

The snitch asked, "Are you still there?"

"Yeah. Let me check this out. I may owe you a favor."

"Make sure it's folding money," instructed the driver as he hung up.

Leduc immediately called Henry the Musician, and said, "I think I've stumbled onto a money-laundering operation nearby."

He relayed the snitch's story.

"Wonder whose it is?" asked Henry.

"I dunno, but they need to clamp down. Boxes are the choice of containers to move money, and cereal boxes are way too obvious to be left behind a bank building."

"Why don't you put the word out to your associates? You might get a marker to put on your books," said Henry.

"Okay. Let's double up. You call your contacts."

Henry still had connections from the old days in the northwest corner of Alabama near Leighton. The State Line Mob, which had controlled the three-state area, had faded into obscurity, but a few of the younger members were still active.

Henry dialed an unlisted number. A hostile voice answered. Henry said, "It's the Musician. Put Shamrock on the line."

"Why?"

"I've got info."

"Hold on."

A minute later, a familiar voice commanded, "Speak."

"Has the line been sprayed?" asked the Musician.

"Yes. No bugs."

Then Henry relayed his news. Shamrock whistled. "I know whose money that is. And they're angry. Very angry. They were shipping a cargo van full of cash, and the rig was seized. They've asked for my help in finding it and who stole it. At least I now know where some of the money is. Since I'm in the area, I expect they'll want me to arrange for the bank to be 'audited.'"

Shamrock was a leftover from the State Line Mob. He was a young man when the gang faded from power. He had been the organization's "bookkeeper" and assigned "audits" to enforcers to take care of any problems the gang faced.

Henry felt a chill. "Attila?" he inquired.

"Yeah. He'll get the job."

"I thought he had retired."

"He's off the road, but he's got a couple of knee-cappers doing the work."

"Are they competent?"

"Their work is to the right of Attila's!"

Henry trembled.

Henry and Attila had served time together in a federal prison. Henry got out first. Attila, a sturdy powerlifter, had one day left on his sentence when he rendered poetic justice to the head of another prisoner with a baseball bat in the exercise yard. The man had snitched to the guards about Attila's hidden stash of pain pills.

The murder, although witnessed by the yard occupants, had occurred unseen by the guards. The warden relied on the testimony of the victim's cellmate and had Attila arrested. Attila was charged with assault with the threat of ten years being added to the remaining one day of his sentence. He got word to his current boss to get hold of Henry for help.

A large amount of cash was delivered to Henry who contacted his criminal lawyer in Southaven, Mississippi. The lawyer got the charges on Attila dropped by locating a lifer who agreed to take the rap in exchange for his elderly mother being put on "easy street."

A week later, Shamrock called the Musician. "I'm your go-between. They want you to handle locating the thief. And hurry."

"What's in it for me?"

"A huge marker and a gunny sack of lettuce."

"Big leaves?" smiled Henry.

"Always!" replied Shamrock. "You'll be reimbursed for your expenses."

"Did you get an order to muscle the banker?"

"Yeah. First, they'll lean on him in a scary way to get his attention. When they confront him, he'll be a pushover for information. The specialists they need are on a job out of the country, and it'll be December before they're available. Those particular guys have the latest gear for remaining silent and unseen."

CHAPTER 25
THE WINGOVER

Henry's telephone was ringing as he stepped into his house with the morning newspaper. It was Trudy, a friend who stripped at the Clothes-Hangers Gentlemen's Club in South Memphis. "I need help!" she urgently requested.

"Okay."

"I need to go away and hide."

The remark piqued Henry's interest. He had loaned Trudy money in the past when she was behind with her bills.

She continued, "I need enough money to survive for a while."

"How much?"

When she told Henry, he whistled, "That's a lot."

"I've got some information that should make it worth your while."

Henry listened while she elaborated. He and her club's owner, the Irishman, had benefited from some of her past tips.

"A fellow came by the club and hired me and Dixie to entertain a truck driver at a rest stop on I-55 south of Gallatin. He said it would be a birthday present for the driver, who was making a regular run from New Orleans. We've done that before, so the request seemed normal. He paid us more than we asked. He said to be sure we had the driver's complete attention."

"Did something go wrong?"

"Sort of. We hooked up with the driver as instructed. We were in a rented van so there would be more room for the party. We teased him, all the while keeping him at bay just like we do our customers at the club. Dixie had his rapt attention when she started twirling her huge, tassel-covered congas in opposite directions. He squealed like a stuck pig, saying he had never seen that before."

Henry smiled at the thought.

Trudy continued, "About the time Dixie's rotations hit overdrive, the driver heard his rig leave the rest stop. He went berserk. He started moaning, 'I'm a dead man now.' We pointed out that if it wasn't recovered, his insurance would pay for it. He exclaimed, 'The cargo can't be replaced!'"

"What happened?"

"We dropped him off at the bus station in Gallatin."

"So, why do you need to get away?"

"I figured that our party with the driver was a set-up so the man who hired us could steal the truck and trailer. I'm scared. That man was in the club this past Saturday, sitting way in the back in the dark, away from the tip rail. He followed me home. I know it was him. As he drove past, I saw a Cade County, Mississippi, tag on his pickup."

"Do you know his name?"

"No. We're never furnished names. He paid in cash."

"Describe him."

Trudy did and added, "He was creepy. He reminded me of that Jabba the Hutt in the movie."

Henry mused, "That describes someone who is known well in the county. He has rigs of his own, so if he stole this particular truck and trailer, it would be for the cargo."

DRIVER'S FLAT

Henry had already learned from Shamrock that a crime syndicate in New Orleans was missing a semi-trailer truck, or at least the cargo. The empty trailer had been found shortly after it was stolen. He shivered when he recalled that a hit had been put out on the driver.

A warm glow came over Henry. This guy had screwed him on a deal a few years back, and he wanted revenge. He decided if he could find the cargo, he could get word to the owner and let the chips fall where they may.

"I'm afraid the heat is on that man, and he wants everyone who knows about his involvement in the heist to disappear," said Trudy.

"You could be right. Meet me at Houston's on Poplar at noon tomorrow. I'll have the money and will buy lunch."

Trudy hesitated, "Enough for Dixie, too?"

"I knew that was coming. Yeah, she's included."

Trudy breathed a sigh of relief. "Henry, you are such a darling!"

On Friday afternoon, Henry the Musician drove to the Skuna River Flying Service outside Baxter. The owner, Frank Berry, was busy servicing his yellow crop sprayer parked off the end of the grass runway. He was being assisted by Bill Cook, a college student majoring in aerospace engineering who also manned the ground radio while Frank was in the air.

Frank, a distinguished, lanky 60-year old, pulled a cowling cover down and fastened the latches. He wiped his hands on a greasy rag as he strode toward Henry. They spoke, and Frank invited Henry into his small office adjacent to the hangar.

The phone rang. As Frank took an order from a cotton farmer, Henry looked at the souvenirs and pictures Frank had fastened to the far wall: a picture of his first plane that he had wrecked on his very first day of spraying; a picture his son-in-law had taken of the plane spraying a field, coming directly at the camera, the wheels just over the tops of the plants; and one picture of Frank standing on the tarmac in flying gear by an F/A-18 Hornet on an air base in Saudia Arabia.

Frank hung the phone up. Henry asked, "How's your lawsuit going?"

"Damn lawyers," scowled Frank. "I'll probably be retired by the time it's settled."

Henry laughed. Last fall Frank had been defoliating cotton with a new Air Tractor over in Chickasaw County when an accident occurred during a wingover. At the end of a pass, he made his usual steep climb and was in the middle of the vertical flat turn to the left that was needed to get the plane flying in the opposite direction, when his propeller came off. (It took Frank thirty minutes at a later deposition to explain what had happened in nine seconds.) He said he knew he had a problem when the windscreen was immediately covered with engine oil, and he heard three thuds rolling underneath the fuselage toward the tail. Flying blind, Frank managed to get the plane out of the turn and landed in an adjacent soybean field. Miraculously, the plane wasn't damaged.

Since Frank had to lease another plane to finish out the season, losses were incurred; not to mention that he also had the wits scared out of him. He went to his lawyer, who sued the manufacturers of the plane, makers of the propeller, the company who had previously reworked the engine, and the firm who had sold him the rig.

In order to proceed with the suit, the propeller had to be found. After the crash, a search was made; but the soybeans and cotton were too high and shielded the ground. Frank thought that after the crops were harvested, the find would be easy. With helpers, he scoured the fields for hours, but no luck.

"Tell me again how you found the prop," smiled Henry.

Frank chuckled. "I fell back to a sure bet. I offered the local Cub Scout troop a hundred dollars and a free meal for all at McDonald's in Tupelo. Those little rascals found it right away in the bean field."

"Where?"

"The nine-foot prop was driven straight into the ground. The top end was barely sticking out of the soybean stubble. If it had been more, the combine header would have snagged the end and caused major damage."

Henry noted, "That mission was right down those scouts' alley."

"What brought you by?" asked Frank, changing the subject.

Henry told him what he wanted. He showed him some aerial maps and marked the area he wanted covered.

"Your flying over this area needs to be as discreet as possible. And I need pictures. Good ones," added Henry.

Frank studied the maps. "This is not on my route to those big cotton fields in Sabougla bottom. My flying is always low and the last time I flew there, the landowner came out and waved a shotgun at me."

"Could you get the photos in one pass?"

"Yeah. I'll need a camera with a fast shutter. My son-in-law has one and can mount it under the belly. But, he's a landman working in the oil fields in South Mississippi and won't be home 'til this weekend. He also has a dark room," explained the pilot. "He can develop the pictures here."

"Look. I'm being pushed to get the photography done. There's a hurry. Could you get that camera rigged up, fly the area, and get me the pics by Monday?"

The urgency of his request made Frank uneasy. He and the Musician went a ways back. He was aware that Henry had done well for himself in the past by being a bird-dog for various shady characters loitering in the wings. This job could pull him toward trouble, so he asked, "What's in it for me?"

DRIVER'S FLAT

"Four big ones, if you find something. And that includes keeping your mouth shut."

Frank whistled. "Boy, I could use that! I've spotted a new limo in Memphis I want. That would finish off my financing."

"Do you need it or want it?" needled the Musician.

Frank replied with a sheepish laugh, "Bingo! Come by about ten Monday morning."

"Hey, I haven't been up at that time in fifty years!" protested Henry.

"Okay. Maybe eleven?" smiled Frank. He knew the Musician to be a nocturnal, party animal.

As he turned to leave, Henry asked, "You can be discreet?"

"That's part of the deal," agreed Frank with a wink.

Henry was standing beside his pink Cadillac at the hangar when Frank landed his plane from an aerial application and taxied to the fuel tanks. Frank ambled into the office, followed by Henry, who was carrying a stuffed paper bag. Frank handed him a stack of black-and-white 8x10's. The pilot sat down in his swivel chair and watched Henry slowly thumb through the photos. He discarded most of them and examined the remaining few very closely.

Henry looked at a series of building shots: a frame house, a barn, and equipment sheds. Several vehicles were parked around the barn, including a cleaning van. Figures could be seen loading bags on a semi-trailer truck backed up to the barn. Faces were upturned toward the plane.

Henry noticed all these pictures were shot at the same altitude. There were three others made at a much lower altitude over a big field. He stared at the photos. Henry realized he had found more than he had hoped for. His instructions for the surveillance of the property hadn't covered this!

He raised an eyebrow and complained, "Wouldn't dropping down that low over this field raise suspicion?"

Frank chuckled. "I wasn't born yesterday. I cut the engine on my approach. When I saw those people watching me, I dived lower over the field and made my engine cough and sputter while starting it back. They'll think I had engine trouble."

Henry laughed to himself. He recollected how a certain woman in Central City got wise to Frank using this technique to suddenly appear in his plane over her swimming pool while she was sunbathing topless. This went on for a while until the lady, with a reputation of being outspoken, gave him a tongue lashing with a string of cuss words in front of a social gathering at the local country club. His embarrassment caused him to alter that particular flight pattern.

"Anyway, I thought that this big field would interest your crony. Or the law," added Frank.

The Musician shot a hard glare toward Frank. "There's four in this bag for you and one for your son-in-law. In case you get a visit about this flight, mum's the word."

"Tell me your name again?"

"Childs. Henry Childs. Also known as 'the Musician.'"

"Never heard of you, buddy."

DRIVER'S FLAT

PART THREE

THE PRESENT - SUMMER

DRIVER'S FLAT

CHAPTER 26
THE LIE DETECTOR TEST

It was now summer in Cade County, Mississippi. The uncomfortable humidity was beginning to creep in. The excitement of the discarded money early in the year had faded, although the hope of more being found had not. Because more important problems had surfaced, the law had temporarily ceased pursuing their search for the origin of the money.

The Monday morning meeting of the Cade County Sheriff's Office in the county seat of Poston began an hour earlier than usual. Today, Sheriff Grady Powers, Chief Deputy Wade Sumrall, and Deputy Sally Ryder had to travel to Jackson for a statewide seminar with other sheriffs and selected staff members. The other deputy present was Sammy Baker. Deputy Jack Early was on his way to the meeting; he had been held up by a state fire marshal officer, who was finishing his report on the Saturday night fire in Baxter. A utility shed, full of used equipment on the grounds of a sawmill site owned by a west coast timber company, had burned to the ground. The state man had arrived on the scene early Sunday morning and had worked the entire day. He had spent the night at the Scott Motel which was across the highway from the mill site.

Just as Sammy finished telling the staff about the assorted DUI's and disturbing the peace arrests, Jack entered the room.

He reported, "Well, it was arson. No doubt about it. You could smell gasoline all around!"

Everyone became attentive. It had been a while since a fire had been started intentionally in Cade County.

Wade Sumrall said, "You know the timber company has insurance to cover the loss. It's a good thing the building was unoccupied."

"I want y'all to find out who set that fire," directed Sheriff Powers. "We don't need a firebug in this county."

"I need to go get some sleep if it's okay with you, Sheriff," said Jack.

"Sure, Jack. You've earned it," said Grady. He instructed Sammy, "I'll leave you in charge while Wade, Sally, and I are in Jackson. Get on the phone after I leave. Call around and see if any of the firemen around the county have noticed anyone behaving suspiciously at past fires. If you have to leave the office, let young Mr. Porter Webb handle any visitors."

Porter "Spider" Webb, an entering college freshman and the nephew of the sheriff's wife, was sitting silently in the corner of the room, listening to the officers talk. He was a summer hire, and his salary was paid by his school's work program. He cheered up at this remark.

The room cleared. Sammy called Dale Edwards, who was the volunteer fire chief in Baxter. His crew was the one who had first responded to the fire. The flames had been so fierce that the Chickenbone Fire Department, located ten miles outside of town, was called for assistance. Sammy chuckled as he dialed the number. The Chickenbone fire truck, upon arrival, had parked at a safe spot. The wind had unexpectedly shifted toward the truck. The red-hot flames scorched the tail feathers of the large red rooster decal on the driver's door. A new paint job would be needed!

Dale Edwards was found at his business. Dale told Sammy that his department had worked five house fires in the winter.

Primer Lusk had been noticed in the crowds of curious onlookers at all five fires. "In fact, he was already on the scene at two of the fires when our truck arrived," said Dale.

Sammy asked, "How did he act?"

"Oh, about like all the other spectators. Except several of us noticed he was the last one to leave each fire," said Dale. "He would offer to help us gather our equipment."

"Do you know of any other potential firebugs?" asked Sammy.

"No. We talk about would-be arsonists at our countywide fire department monthly meetings. No other name has surfaced. I'm not saying Primer is starting fires. We just noticed him being a regular on our calls."

"I understand, but I think I need to bring him in and eliminate him as a suspect. Do you know where I might find him?"

"Try the Shell station. He repairs flats there and does other odd jobs. He's a good worker even though his brain is slow."

The conversation had been broadcasting on the speaker, and Spider Webb intently soaked up every word.

After the call, Sammy sank into deep thought for a few minutes. He stood up, put on his western hat, looked at Spider and asked, "Son, can you run this office while I look for Primer Lusk?"

Spider eagerly said, "Oh, sure!"

Sammy said, "I'm going to interview Primer when I bring him back. I'll probably need another witness. Do you have a buddy that could come here for that?"

"I'll cover that," said Spider.

By the time Sammy was getting into his vehicle, Spider was on the phone calling his friends, Derbo Swaney and Charley Luke. He knew both would be in the poolroom in Central City.

Derbo and Charley had been one of ten teams hired by the local county agent, Mr. Jules, to take soil samples from nearby farms. The samples would be sent to the local land-grant college for analysis of fertilizer needs of each farm. The duo would get one sample in the morning and then head to a hidden spot to chew tobacco and pitch washers until noon. After lunch, the morning's episode was repeated and continued all week. At the end of the first week, this team's production was the worst of all. They were scolded by Mr. Jules in front of their fellow workers, and the scolding made the two very angry.

On Monday, they headed to a field and filled all of their soil sample boxes from one spot in a few minutes. They had the rest of the week to pitch washers. At the Friday meeting, they were in first place, by far. Mr. Jules was so pleased that he gave them two days off.

This job was completed by the end of June, so Derbo and Charley had the remainder of the summer to loaf.

Spider dialed the number. Eck was in the restroom, so Derbo, who was the nearest person to the phone, grabbed it and answered in a gruff voice, "Potshot's Poolroom. Nobody racks our balls!"

Spider sniggered, "Hey, you deadbeat. This is Deputy Webb. You and Charley get your tails up to the sheriff's office, pronto! I've got work for y'all."

Fifteen minutes later, both pals swaggered past the 911 operator into the office. Spider had helped himself to Grady's desk, was leaned back in the leather chair, and had his feet up. He had already fished two deputy badges out of the top drawer. Spider had the two men stand in front of the desk and raise their right hands. He quipped, "Do each of you promise to cause as much strife and turmoil as possible during the term of your office?"

Derbo and Charley did high fives saying, "You got it!"

They immediately searched every drawer and closet in sight to see what they contained. These three had just graduated from high school to the relief of every teacher on the staff, especially Mrs. Denton, the math teacher. They had taken "horseplay" to the highest level during their four years at Central City High.

After their office search ended, they took turns on the telephone calling buddies with threats to arrest them for past pranks. When they tired of the calls, they began to practice hand-cuffing. Derbo tried to wrestle down Charley, who was bigger, and, in the process knocked an Oriental lamp off a stand. The lamp broke into three large pieces. Spider gleefully announced, "That was a Ming Dynasty lamp. Y'all will never get through paying for that!"

Some glue and clear tape was found, and, luckily, they were able to fit the pieces together without the cracks being visible. Then the kitchen was raided. They ate all the food in the refrigerator, spraying each other and the walls with cool-whip and soft drinks, which squirted from shaken-up bottles. The boys came to their senses when they heard Sammy's car crunch gravel in the parking lot.

They quickly cleaned the kitchen and were sitting in chairs against the wall when Sammy came in with Primer Lusk in tow. Primer was a stocky black man, about forty years old. He was wearing khaki work clothes, a baseball cap, and worn leather shoes. He talked very loudly and came across as being eager to be accepted. He had lived all his life in Cade County and was a hard worker. He was known to succumb to the temptations of alcohol from time to time. Primer wasn't a social drinker, so his benders were hardcore.

Sammy looked around, and seeing badges pinned on the boys, chuckled to himself. He announced to Primer, "These are my summer deputies. Is it okay if they stay in the room while me and you talk?"

Primer smiled broadly, "Yas, sir!"

DRIVER'S FLAT

Sammy told Primer to take a seat in front of his desk. Sammy went into a series of questions about the mill fire the past weekend. Primer admitted to being at the fire but denied having any involvement with it or knowing who might have been. Sammy felt his answers bordered on being evasive. This interview went on for some time and Spider, Derbo, and Charley absorbed every aspect of the questioning procedure. Finally, Sammy gave up in disgust.

Spider intervened, "Mr. Sammy, would you give me a shot at asking Primer some questions?"

Sammy mulled over the consequences of Spider being involved. If Primer accidentally admitted to being involved in the fires, the confession might not hold up in court, since Spider wasn't a real deputy. But a confession, at this point, was unlikely. So he threw up his hands and uttered, "Yeah. Go ahead."

Spider moved to Sheriff Powers' desk. He placed a chair at the left end and told Primer to sit in it facing him. He asked, "Primer, have you ever seen either me or my two associate deputies before?"

Primer looked the other two over carefully and answered, "No. I ain't never seed any of y'all befo."

Spider, with tongue in cheek, replied, "Well, we are in a special area of law enforcement and are helping the sheriff this summer. Have you ever taken a lie detector test?"

Primer squirmed in his seat, "Naw, sir. But I heard 'bout them."

"Would you mind taking one?"

"Well, I ain't lying, so I guess so."

Spider pointed to an office calculator sitting on a shelf in an open closet and said, "Deputy Derbo, you and Deputy Charley bring that lie detector over here and hook it up on my desk."

With their heads turned so Primer couldn't see them smiling, they retrieved the machine. One placed it on the desk near Primer, and the other plugged it into an outlet. Spider took a blood pressure monitor that he had discovered earlier from the bottom drawer of the desk and started to untangle the cuff and tubing.

Primer's body began to tense. "How long is this gonna to take?"

Spider replied, "Oh, about thirty minutes."

Primer announced, "Then I'm gonna to need a sweet water and a Moon Pie to do this!"

Sammy had to bite his tongue to not laugh out loud. He was beginning to see where this was going. He assured Primer, "I'll cover you on that, Primer. But you'll have to wait until I carry you home."

Primer contended, "If we wait that long, I wants doubles!"

Spider fitted the cuff loosely on Primer's bicep. He unplugged the calculator from the wall, ran the cord under the cuff, and replugged it. Then he turned the machine on. The screen lit up, and as Spider hit different keys, the display lights turned from green to orange to red. The machine had been put on the market by the ACME Corporation five years ago with the intent for it to be a sales leader. It was innovative because ACME's technology permitted a negative result to be displayed in red, a positive result to be displayed in green, and the previous number entered before a total to be displayed in orange.

However, the technology was defective, and the colors were reliably inconsistent. So the company had no choice but to write off this particular venture as a loss. A staff accountant pointed out that ACME could get a further tax credit by donating the unsold machines to charity. Thus, every law enforcement agency and high school in the nation found themselves recipients of those machines.

The machine was known to students as the "Traffic Light." Spider, Derbo, and Charley had used these calculators in Mr. Dickerson's high school office machine course.

Spider began to pump the meter's bulb. As the cuff tightened on Primer's arm, his body stiffened and his eyes began to roll. Spider let the pressure off. Primer relaxed. Then Spider pumped it tighter than before and asked, "What's your name?"

Primer bleated, "Primer Lusk!" He saw Spider hit a key and the machine displayed a line of sevens in green.

Spider then asked, "Have you ever eyeballed a pretty woman?"

Primer exclaimed, "No. Never!" He saw Spider hit a key and a line of zeros appeared in red.

He stammered, " I means 'yes'! I means 'no'! I means not a married woman."

Spider tightened the cuff even more. Primer wailed, "Oh, man! I don't knows what I means!"

Spider responded in a calm, reassuring voice, "Now, Primer. I'm your friend. But this machine is not. It knows a lie when it hears one. And, if I pump this cuff more than I have already and hit all these buttons at one time, it can even read your mind. You don't want that, do you?"

"Sir! Not that! Just stays with them questions. I don't needs them lights up in my haid. Please, Mr. Spider," moaned Primer.

Spider proceeded with a series of questions. When he quit, everyone in the room was convinced that Primer was not involved with the mill fire but, to the amazement of Deputy Baker, he confessed to knowing about two crimes that the sheriff's office didn't even know had been committed.

The first secret crime was about a consumer shakedown that had just begun. Jermaine, a local crack-head, had gone to a certain retail store in Oxford a few weeks ago. He bought two expensive items, paid for them, and saved the receipt. The next day, he returned to the store with Primer. Jermaine placed two more of the same items in his buggy, went through the self-check and bagged them, un-scanned. Primer, as instructed, filled his buggy and scanned and paid for all the items, except for a single candy bar that he placed on the bottom part of the buggy.

The two pushed their buggies side-by-side, past the door alarm which was triggered by the unscanned candy bar. Primer stopped, but Jermaine moved on waving the previous day's receipt in the air for the checker to observe. Primer stuttered that the candy bar must have dropped to the buggy's bottom without being seen. The employee took the candy but let him leave.

Primer admitted that Jermaine was still hoaxing the store but had dropped him as an accomplice because Primer had demanded too much beer for future trips.

The second crime was puzzling. It had originated in nearby Gallatin County but had ended in Cade County. Primer had been sitting on the wooden bench outside the Shell station in Baxter, smoking a Camel, when a late model, Ford pickup with loud pipes and Tennessee plates pulled in for gas. The driver got out and started the pump. The passenger spied Primer and approached him. "Say, brother. Where can me and my buddy find a party?"

Primer looked them over. They were young and well dressed. Both had fake Rolex watches on their wrists and several gold chains around their necks. They reeked of cash. He proceeded to tell them about The Arcade, a beer joint across the county line in Gallatin County that catered to black patrons.

One of them asked, "Do they have music and women?"

DRIVER'S FLAT

Primer beamed. "Sho nuff! It's always loaded with hos, and tonight there's a band!"

"Why don't you get in and show us how to get to that place? We'll buy you some beer."

Primer gleefully crawled into the back seat of the club cab pickup, and they sped away.

Primer asked, "What are you city brothers doin' down here?"

One winked at the other and replied seriously, "Oh, we had to make a visit to our 'uncle's' farm below Central City and pick up some hay to mulch our tomato plants."

"You boys don't look likes nobody who plants a garden," replied Primer, suspiciously.

One laughed. "If you saw the kind of tomatoes we plant, you would understand."

Primer joined the merriment even though he did not understand why that reply was so funny.

The three partied a while at The Arcade, flirting with the women and enjoying the blues music. Around midnight, the strangers decided to leave. Primer volunteered to show them a shortcut back to Baxter.

The route was along a gravel road that ran around the back of Gallatin Lake, a huge Corp of Engineers' flood control lake built around 1954. At this time of year, the lake level was normal. As the pickup moved along, the driver spied a campfire at the end of a field road near the water's edge. The driver also noticed that this was an isolated area. They had seen no other traffic during their drive.

They passed down the road out of sight of the campfire and turned around. As they moved back up the road, the driver turned his lights off, eased quietly along the dirt road a ways and stopped. The campfire was about a quarter of a mile distant across an open field. The driver and his companion pulled pistols from under the truck seat and got out. They

DRIVER'S FLAT

commanded Primer to come along. By this time, Primer was too drunk to comprehend what was about to happen, so he meekly followed them on the field road.

The three quietly sneaked close to the campfire and stopped to case the situation.

They could see a man seated on a block of wood with his back propped against the trunk of a huge oak tree. He had a mug of coffee in his hand and was staring into the hissing flames. The skinny man was very pale and his blonde hair was balled in a knot behind his head. A serpent tattoo wound around his left arm with its head positioned at his wrist. The snake's upper fang was on the forefinger and the lower fang was on his thumb. The man was absent-mindedly clacking his thumb against the finger, mimicking a snake strike. The three observed him a while. There was no vehicle to be seen, but they noticed an expensive 4-wheeler parked in the edge of the firelight. A trailer loaded with a bass boat and 250 HP Mercury motor was hooked to the ATV. The two city brothers whispered their plan to rob the camper of his gear and any valuables he might have on him.

They edged into the firelight. Primer uneasily hung back in the darkness. He was scared of snakes. Even fake ones. He had begun to sober up when he realized that his comrades were going to rob the camper. Primer felt antsy about the scene; something just wasn't right. The atmosphere seemed tense.

The camper looked up and spoke, "Hello. Y'all want some coffee?"

The dudes ignored the invitation, pulled out their firearms, and one replied, "Nah! We want your money!"

The camper calmly stared. One brother asked, "Where is your gun? You got to have one being by yourself way out here."

Primer began to slide back. That guy was too composed. He noticed the man wasn't scared at all.

The camper looked them over as he tightly squeezed his inked digits together and replied, "Why do I need a gun when I have noise?"

"Huh?" the bigger dude asked. "What do you mean?"

The camper peered at them and barked loudly, "Listen!"

The brothers looked around frantically. Then they heard it. High up in the tree above the reaches of the firelight, the sound of a bolt of an assault rifle going forward with a round, reverberated!

Then all hell broke loose! A muscular man dressed in camo dropped from the tree branches, firing from his waist toward the brothers as he descended. The three fled, Primer leading the way toward the truck.

Primer excitedly told the deputies, "Man, I was running! And them red hornets was zipping all around us."

Sammy thought to himself, "Tracers!" He asked, "Primer. What were you thinking?"

Primer exclaimed, "I wasn't thinkin'. I was sanging!"

Sammy chuckled. "What were you singing?"

He cackled, "My favorite song, '*Feet Don't Fail Me Now*!'"

The deputies howled at this revelation.

Sammy asked, "What happened next?"

"Well, I sailed into the back of the pickup and landed in a pile of loose, funny smelling, hay. Them dudes got into the front and took off fast."

"Did they take you home?"

"Nah. I walked."

"Walked?" asked Sammy.

"Yeah. About the time we got to Cole's Creek, about two miles away, I felt something bump into the back of the pickup."

"What?"

"I don't know. It was a dark night and I didn't see or hear nuttin' come up behind us."

DRIVER'S FLAT

Spider asked, "What happened?"

"The pickup went off the bridge into the creek. But I didn't. I jumped and went into orbit like them space mens do. I landed on the bridge."

"What happened to the city dudes?"

"I don't know and I don't care! I hit the bushes to get away. I got lost, and it took me all night to come out on a road."

"Where did you come out?"

"Oh, when I seed it on the side of the road, I knowed where I was!"

"Where?" asked Sammy.

Primer chattered, "Down there at the county line crossroads on the Gallatin highway at that ranch where that tin sign is with that big Black Angus bull on it that is looking at you no matter which way you are coming from!"

Sammy made a note to call the Gallatin County sheriff's office to report the incident and to ask for a drive-by of the campsite.

DRIVER'S FLAT

CHAPTER 27
PAGE 63

Bespectacled, unshaven Winslow Percy, the editor of *The Whisperer,* was glumly staring at the letter that Clytee wanted to discuss in her next column. He was beginning to regret ever allowing her page to be a part of his paper. He was from an old family that was well known in the fields of journalism and publishing. Winslow's paper had consistently won national awards in different categories. His hard work in reporting news accurately had earned him an impeccable reputation.

He had to admit that Clytee's column was so popular that the paper's circulation had tripled. He was even getting subscribers from three states away. Last week, he had a call from a large chain that wanted to syndicate Clytee's column.

Winslow read the letter for the fifth time. Two days ago, the first round of thick catalogs from a national retailer had arrived in Cade County. A busybody, eagle-eyed Joyce, had thumbed through her copy. Her question to Clytee was, "Why is the catalog company sending out porn to our county? Look at the model on page 63."

Clytee had left the letter on his desk for approval. He had no idea what this was about. He had just returned from a weekend food tour of restaurants in Mobile and on the Gulf Coast with a local medicus and two gourmand friends.

Curious, he retrieved his catalog from a stack of unopened mail and turned to the referenced page. There was a handsome, bare-chested male model at the bottom of the page, clad only in white boxer shorts.

Winslow stared! Just past the end of the shorts on the model's left thigh was a round, vague blur. He looked at the spot. Over and over. He concluded that you couldn't say, "It was," and you couldn't say, "It wasn't."

Winslow had gone around town checking out the page in other catalogs in case there had been a misprint in his. They were all the same. He realized that publishing the letter would bring in tons of criticism from his readers, most of whom were strait-laced.

Shortly, Clytee walked into his office expecting a warm reception about this week's letter. As she sat across his desk, Winslow frowned at her and announced. "Clytee, I can't print this letter."

Crestfallen, Clytee demanded, "Why?"

"It's too risqué for Cade County."

"No more than the jokes I tell."

"Well, you tell them to your circle of friends. You know, 'birds of a feather, flock together.' My paper circulates among a wider audience."

"But, it's the best one yet."

"I don't care. I'm not printing it."

Clytee rose in a huff and declared, "Okay. Have it your way. I quit."

Caught by surprise, Winslow began to sweat. With her gone, he could sense that his circulation would drop to pre-Clytee levels, or below.

"Now, wait a minute. Can't we work this out?"

Clytee thought, "Now I have him under my control." News about the catalog was already furiously spreading around the county by word of mouth - a faster conduit than the sluggish printing and distribution of a newspaper. When this week's edition hits the stands, the news would be old. Winslow was probably right about irate letters flooding the doors. That could overshadow her column.

When the news of page 63 reached the coffee shops, the drinkers had quickly divided into two sides: the "it is" side versus the "it ain't" side.

Heated arguments arose. Friendships were strained and a few dissolved - all over who was right and who was wrong about what the page portrayed. Irate customers of the mail order company who hadn't received their catalog appeared at the counters of their respective post offices and accused the clerks of stealing their mail. The most popular story told was about Little Ben Weaver strolling into the busy supermarket in Central City and announcing to a striking, middle-aged checker at the front register, "Melba, the company is recalling all their catalogs."

Melba, known to speak her thoughts to friends and strangers alike, shouted so loudly she could be heard all over the store and down the street, "Nobody is getting my catalog! Especially page 63!"

Clytee coyly replied, "Maybe so. I want to do the weekly arrest report in addition to my column."

Winslow was stunned. Why would she want to do that? That was so mundane. Maybe she wants that task so she could "unreport" embarrassing arrests of any of her friends.

Clytee added, "And I want to be the reporter who attends court trials." Being seen in the courtroom should encourage more letters to be sent her way.

What could it hurt? Winslow could visualize her being the center of attention among the spectators at a trial.

He reluctantly agreed with hope that he had not let the genie out of the bottle, and meekly asked, "I guess you want a raise?"

Clytee smiled, reached over the desk and patted Winslow's hand, "No, Hon. I have plenty of money. I just need attention, especially male."

DRIVER'S FLAT

CHAPTER 28
THE DUMP

Cecil Shaw, a land trader from Millport, Alabama, parked his pickup under the shade of a red oak tree. He was in the middle of a large tract of woods on the south side of Cade County. A college kid, who was majoring in forestry hired by Cecil to help cruise timber this summer, was with him.

Cecil's GPS had brought him through a pine plantation to the south boundary line of a parcel of land covered with hardwoods. He had purchased the property from a business partner, sight unseen. He wanted to verify the board feet of the different species listed on a prior timber tally he held in his hand.

Cecil was unfamiliar with these woods. He examined an aerial map of his tract. On the north was another expansive pine plantation. Cecil could see that the same dirt road he used to enter the woods ran through the center of his tract and continued a mile along a ridge to a county gravel road. He could tell no one had traveled this road since the last rain.

He and his helper inventoried the woods on the east side of the dirt road. When they came up to the dirt road, they noticed tractor tire tracks coming from the north. Trailer tracks were between the wider tractor tracks. Curious, they followed the marks for about a hundred yards to where they veered down through brush into a hollow. There was no road here, but the tractor had ridden down small bushes, making its own trail. As they descended the slope, they ran into a peculiar odor, which became stronger as the men neared a small creek with steep banks.

They could see where the tractor had made a wide turn at the edge of the creek bank to head back up the hill.

Cecil and his helper peered into the deep cut of the creek. Cecil exclaimed, "What the heck?"

The creek was full of commercial dog food. The guys stared! There were tons of it.

The helper blurted, "What in the world is going on?"

Apparently, the dog food had been dumped there at several different times. It had been aged by the weather into distinct layers, which could be seen from an angle. The top layer was a day fresh, but the bottom layer was months-old.

Cecil and his helper sat down on a nearby log and discussed their find. There were no dead animals around, so the dog food was not contaminated. They reasoned that a factory needed a clandestine disposal site and had found a landowner in the area who would handle it for a fee. But why? Maybe to dodge a costly EPA inspection? Had management used a defective formula that would initiate a recall?

The helper wise-cracked, "It wouldn't have surprised me to find a new Dollar General store in the middle of these woods. But a creek full of dog food?"

Cecil's six-foot frame shook with mirth!

Forgetting their strange find, they left the creek and finished their tabulation of trees. Cecil decided to go home by following the woods road to the county road. They got out of the truck and inspected its surface to see which direction the tractor had traveled, but the tracks had been swept away by recent traffic.

They discussed what to do. Cecil replied, "There is nothing illegal. Dog food is biodegradable and the coyotes should be thrilled about this bonus feast. On the other hand, I really don't like someone helping themselves to my land without talking to me."

"Why don't you report it to some authority?" asked the helper.

"I'll make some calls. I don't know anyone over here. Those pines we came through belong to Weyerhaeuser. I'll give their fieldman a call about who I can contact. I need to talk to someone at Weyerhaeuser anyway about permission to use their road when I sell my trees and log them out."

"What are you going to do with your money?"

"I'll buy another condo in Gulf Shores. One more will get me to my goal of seven."

"Why seven?"

"I rent my condos by the week. With seven rented, I can count on getting one condo's weekly rent in one day. Makes me feel good," smirked Cecil.

"Man, I hope someday I'm as rich as you are!" exclaimed the young helper.

DRIVER'S FLAT

CHAPTER 29
CADARETTA ROAD

Dusk was falling on the August day, and Deputy Sammy Baker had the night shift along with his three deputy interns. They were busy cleaning the various firearms housed in the office.

Seated in front of him was a distressed Lou Bertha Eason. She was sweating and breathing heavily. When Sammy asked the reason of her visit, she spoke loudly, "I was out in the woods scouting for muscadines to pick once they get ripe. When I got back to my car parked on the road, I saw all fo' tires were flat. All at the same time! That ain't natural."

Sammy gawked and asked, "Where were you parked?"

"Down yonder on the Cadaretta Road, next to Mr. Shifty McCord's farm by Shutispear Creek."

"That's not the Cadaretta Road."

"How come?"

"Cadaretta is across the line in Webster County."

"Well, it may be. But that same road goes there after you make a few turns."

Sammy persisted, "Lou Bertha, according to your logic that highway outside the office could be called the Denver highway because you could get there from here!"

"Don't you joke with me!" warned Lou Bertha. "I'se not in a good mood right now."

"Okay. Who was with you?"

"Just me."

"How did you get home?"

"I dialed my grandson, James Henry, on my cell phone to come get me. It took him a while 'cause he was finishin' cleanin' up his car. And he brung me straight here. I ain't putting up with this rubbish!" She made a fist and waved it in the air.

She continued, "And I gots to tell you something. I got turned around in them woods, and on my way out, I come into a corner of one of Mr. Shifty's fields. I ain't no fool. As far as I could see was ...."

The phone rang. Sammy picked it up to hear the excited voice of Bill Marter, the sheriff of neighboring Webster County. He told Sammy that he had a car pulled over on his segment of the Cadaretta Road near the county line.

He exclaimed, "I'm on to something huge. Meet me here immediately!"

As Sammy grabbed his hat and rushed out the door, he told Lou Bertha, "Finish your report with my three young deputies, Spider Webb, Derbo Swaney, and Charley Luke."

They had been absorbed with Lou Bertha's story and had stopped cleaning the firearms.

Thirty minutes later, Sammy pulled in behind Sheriff Marter's SUV. The sheriff and a deputy had three young men handcuffed and seated on the ground by their older Chevy. Both of its back doors were open.

Bill waved Sammy to the car with his flashlight and said, "Look inside."

DRIVER'S FLAT

Sammy gasped! The floorboard and back seats were filled with green, mature marijuana stalks: whole plants with the dirty roots still attached.

Bill instructed the larger of the youths, "Tell this man where y'all got these plants."

The boy chattered nervously, "Over yonder in Cade County on Mr. McCord's farm. The whole place is covered up with marijuana. It's growing all over them hills and branch bottoms."

Bill chuckled. "They got greedy. Instead of grabbing some leaves and pods, they just pulled up whole stalks."

"Why did you pull them over?" asked Sammy as he pulled Sheriff Marter to the side.

Bill winked. "No reason. I just wanted to warn them that some horses had got out of a pasture back down the road and were milling around. When I shined my light in the car and saw the marijuana in plain sight, I had to make the arrest!"

When Sammy got back to his office, Lou Bertha was gone. The three deputies were smiling. Spider handed him her report, already typed.

They watched him read the pages. She told about seeing acres of marijuana. She added her thoughts that Shifty was the one who had flattened her tires as a warning not to come back.

Sammy told the boys about Sheriff Marter's arrest and added, "Lou Bertha's report confirms there's a major grow on the McCord place."

The young deputies shifted in their chairs. They knew a raid was forthcoming, and they hoped to be included.

Sammy looked sternly at the boys and warned, "If y'all let this news get out, I'll personally knock a white-chalked dog turd out of each one of you!"

The three snickered, and Spider reported, "Lou Bertha said she wasn't staying away from Shifty. That she was going to be all over him like 'white on rice.'"

Sammy called Sheriff Powers at home about the grow. He could feel excitement coming through the phone lines.

Grady exclaimed, "Yeah! We'll raid that farm as soon as I can get a search warrant. Let's see how many votes sheriff's candidate Shifty McCord will get while his butt sits in jail."

DRIVER'S FLAT

CHAPTER 30
THE RAID

On the following Sunday night, the sheriff's office was overflowing with law enforcement personnel. All the chairs were occupied; bodies were leaning against the walls. The crowd had spilled into the hall. Present were all the deputies, state narcotics officers, troopers with the Mississippi Highway Patrol, and officers from the police departments of Vena, Baxter, and Central City. Everybody wanted a piece of this action!

Cade County Sheriff Grady Powers was in charge. He presented a tentative plan to raid Shifty's farm. Each person was assigned a specific duty. The narcotics officers had three helicopters at their disposal. An agreement was reached that they would fly over the McCord farm Monday afternoon to spot any marijuana. They would radio the location; the nearby officers would swoop to the spot.

Grady spoke, "It may take y'all a while. That's a 600-acre farm of many scattered cotton and soybean fields."

Deputy Baker pointed to the field on an aerial photo that Lou Bertha had approached on her trip out of the woods and then told one of the pilots, "Try this spot first. There may not be as much out there as those kids over in Webster County said."

"As soon as I have a confirmed visual, I'll radio the command center," said the lead pilot.

"We all need to move quickly when we get the word," cautioned Grady. "Everybody needs to keep as quiet as possible."

The officers and agents began to file from the room. As Derbo and Charley moved past, Grady commanded, "Hold up. Didn't you boys notice anything suspicious on Shifty's farm when y'all took soil samples out there this summer?"

Derbo was reluctant to answer. His feet shifted and he stammered, "Naw. His was the only farm that we didn't go on."

"How come? That job required samples be taken from all farms."

Charley responded, "They were. But Shifty took them for us."

Grady asked, "How did that happen?"

"Oh, we were headed to his farm one morning when Shifty came out of nowhere and stopped us where his field road left the highway. He told us to give him the sample boxes and he would fill them," said Charley, who was ready to blame anybody for their shoddy work.

Derbo added, "Yeah. That made us happy because that got us out of an all-day job. And Shifty pulled a bottle of Jack from his pickup toolbox and laughed. 'Y'all go fishing and take this mosquito medicine with you!'"

The first helicopter found two fields of marijuana where Lou Bertha had been. Agents poured from their respective hideouts. They apprehended several workers and went on the lookout for Shifty. He was caught as he tried to flee from a hay shed in his pickup.

The initial field had 700 plants. A second field in a peach orchard located at the end of a pasture had almost 1200 plants. The agents also discovered a maze of trip wires hooked up to a sensor detector in this field.

While the agents were pulling up these plants, one of the helicopters flew out over another patch of marijuana. It took all members of the raid the rest of the afternoon to pull up the plants.

The next morning the raid continued with many more fields being discovered. By the end of the day, the total plant count was 14,190! All, except a small amount held for transport to the crime lab for evidence, was put into a huge pile and burned. It took 300 gallons of diesel fuel to destroy the marijuana.

By this time, the heavy plume of smoke had caught the attention of neighbors who quickly spread the news. Sheriff Powers had anticipated that curious onlookers would appear. Since he didn't want interference with his raid, he blocked off the two roads that ran either to, or through, Shifty's farm.

On a hill overlooking the farm buildings, he assigned his summer deputies to man the roadblock. They positioned their squad car diagonally on the road.

Soon, vehicles started to park in a line on each side of the gravel road. The occupants exited and hurried to the barrier like they were going to miss something.

An alternate lifestyle female, wearing indecent denim shorts, with a ring in her nose and a tattoo on her left thigh depicting a skull holding a red rose stem crossways in its mouth, stared at the smoke and exclaimed, "What a cruel waste!"

DRIVER'S FLAT

An older unshaven man wearing a straw hat tucked one hand inside his blue overalls and muttered as he scratched away, "I wish the wind would blow that smoke this way!"

A deacon from a nearby country Baptist church, with his wife and two children at his side, thoughtfully commented, "I don't think Shifty is going to be elected sheriff!"

Two more bystanders were Andy, the druggist in Baxter, and J.R., his fellow pharmacist from Central City. They had ridden to the drug raid together. On the way, they had joked that their attendance should earn each at least a day's credit of continuing education.

One of the spectators was Wes Jarvis, the local USDA loan officer who held an upside-down lien on the farm. He was wringing his hands and was heard moaning, "What a mess! I'll never be able to get out from under the red tape that will come from Washington over this episode!"

J. R., standing nearby, tried to console him by saying, "At least you're not involved with the farming operations."

The words were to no avail. Wes Jarvis blurted, "But I just know the law will try to connect me when they start seizure proceedings."

J. R. cackled when Wes exclaimed, "Liquor has never touched my lips, but I may get drunk tonight!"

Shifty was brought before a justice who had him placed in the county jail under a $1 million bond. As Shifty was putting on his jail-issued, orange "pumpkin suit," he laughed so much he shook. "I'll only be here until I'm elected sheriff! Elected officials are immune from sentences while they're in office."

DRIVER'S FLAT

CHAPTER 31
THE PRE-TRIAL HEARING

Shifty had hired Loophole Larry to represent him on the marijuana charges. Not because Loophole was a savvy criminal defense lawyer. Not because his fees would be way under those charged by a big shot lawyer. But simply because they had been high school classmates.

Larry had represented Shifty on several civil matters before moving to the coast. He had discovered that Shifty could be belligerent and difficult. Larry would give advice on his issues, to which Shifty would agree. Then Shifty would leave his office and proceed to take opposite action.

One time, Shifty had complained that his insurance company wouldn't pay when his combine burned. Larry had called the adjuster and got hot with him and threatened a bad-faith suit for not paying. The adjuster asked for the machine's serial number and promptly informed Larry that the claim had been paid a year ago!

Not really wanting to represent him on the drug charge, Loophole had quoted an excessive fee to carry the case through a trial. Shifty had mulled over the amount. Without saying a word, he left Larry's office and returned the next day to pay the entire fee. In cash.

DRIVER'S FLAT

Larry put a lot of effort into the case. He had researched the law as it applied to the particular facts, interviewed witnesses, and investigated the background of every person on the jury pool list.

Loophole filed a motion to quash the indictment. It was to be heard on the 2nd day of the October term of the Cade County Circuit Court, which was a Tuesday. On Monday, the clerk called Larry and told him that there had been a mix-up. A criminal jury trial was to start that morning; Judge Haller said to come after one o'clock. He would send the jury out at first opportunity and would hear Larry's motion.

At 1:15, a speeding BMW with Shelby County, Tennessee, plates bearing the letters *ISUEU* came to a screeching halt in the courthouse parking lot. Thirty-year-old Stanley Robbs, with the law firm of Janes, Knobly, and Stilt, of Memphis, grabbed his expensive, monogrammed leather briefcase, jumped from the car, and ran inside the courthouse. The lanky, red-headed lawyer was not in a good mood.

Stanley, the only son from a rich family in Baltimore, had been with the Memphis firm for five years. He didn't stand in well with the office staff because of his egotistical attitude. They considered him arrogant and spoiled. The secretaries went out of their way to make his life difficult.

He had planned to be on the greens of his club in East Memphis, but this morning he had been urgently called into the office of senior partner Povall Janes. "We've been hired by a high-powered client in New Orleans to help a local district attorney prosecute some redneck named Shifty McCord down in Mississippi. He got caught raising a lot of marijuana on his farm. He's already been indicted and a motion hearing to quash is today after one o'clock. He has a local attorney named Larry Lawrence. I know you interned with a district attorney in law school, and you're the only lawyer in the firm available today that knows anything about criminal law," explained Povall.

"I didn't know a private attorney could help prosecute a criminal case."

"They can in Mississippi."

"What do you want me to do?" asked Stanley.

"Go down there and sit in. That lawyer is probably just going through the motions with this hearing. It's rare to succeed in quashing an indictment. And such a waste if he wins, because the state just re-indicts."

"Why us?" puzzled Stanley.

Povall squirmed. Stanley didn't need to know why the client insisted that Shifty should go to prison. "This client has used us before on civil and criminal matters. They're wiring a huge retainer this afternoon," admitted Povall.

Stanley nodded. He could sense importance.

Povall continued, "This case is in Cade County." He said with emphasis.

Stanley reddened. That was where he and his firm had gotten their ears boxed by Archie Baker last year in the Joab McMath will contest. The whole group had limped home to Memphis with their tails between their legs.

Povall smiled with reassurance. "This time it's in the circuit court with a different judge who doesn't know us. So you behave." He pointed his finger as he continued, "When this matter goes to trial, all our heavyweights will be there."

Stanley looked at his watch and jumped up. "I need to hit the road," he moaned. He already knew the travel time to Poston.

"We've not been able to contact McCord's lawyer. The clerk said he's a loose cannon but is never late for court. So meet him at the courthouse and see if he will back off."

"What does Lawrence look like?" asked Stanley.

"I called my longtime attorney friend in Tupelo, Gary Nettleton, to inquire about Lawrence. I found that he is called 'Loophole,' for having been successful in squirming out of hopeless legal situations."

"That's neat," replied Stanley.

"Gary knows all about him. He wears his curly dark hair in a retro haircut. He has a rough face. His trademark is the way he wears his tie. He loops it around his collar one time and flips the long end over the short end without completing the usual knot. He also chain-smokes in the courtroom."

"I thought smoking was prohibited in all courtrooms," said Stanley.

"According to Gary, Loophole ignores the signs, smokes when he feels the need, and gets away with it."

As Stanley left the office, Janes called, "Stanley, neither McCord nor his lawyer knows yet that we've been hired."

Stanley stopped, "That's weird."

"That's what I thought. Someone up the line wants him sent to the pen. For a long time. I've been firmly instructed that we're not to allow the district attorney to accept a plea."

"Aha! He's to play the 'quiet game'?" responded Stanley.

Povall Janes smiled at Stanley's perception.

Stanley entered the hall of the courthouse and slid through the door at the back, which was one of two entrances for spectators. The area was about three-fourths full. A jury trial was in progress. He quietly walked toward the rail which divided the spectator area from the front of the room and took a seat on the third pew. Against the left wall was a space for the clerk and her staff. Against the opposite wall was the jury box. And against the front wall was the judge's bench. The defense table was on the left, facing the prosecution table which had the jury to its back.

Stanley studied all the people behind the rail and didn't see anyone who remotely resembled Loophole's description. He wondered if Loophole was running late. He recognized the prosecutor as a lawyer he had opposed in a matter in Holly Springs a few years ago. At the defense table sat a young lawyer, who he surmised to be the local public defender. By him sat Thomas, a rugged man with a weathered face, jeans, T-shirt, leather vest, tattoos, and an Outlaw biker do-rag. Thomas was looking wildly around the courtroom with a bad-tempered frown. His mean eyes locked on Stanley, who quickly averted his gaze. Stanley now remembered walking by a group of Harleys, parked side by side in a line against a curb, as he left his car.

Stanley let a minute go by before he gained enough courage to peep forward. He noticed that the front rows on each side of the aisle were filled by burly, unwashed men wearing leather biker jackets, sitting shoulder to shoulder. Then he glanced at the jury and noticed that no one was paying any attention to the testimony of the prosecutor's witness. All of them, and the judge, were staring in the distance at a spot on the far wall. Stanley's jaw dropped. High on a shelf, a TV screen with the volume turned down showed a baseball playoff game between the Cardinals and the Giants! Now he understood the defendant's mood.

While he was absorbing this spectacle, an attractive, elegant, older woman slipped into the middle of the room behind him. Clytee Lott. Around her neck was a leather badge holder, containing a square of stiff white paper that read "Press." She had never been to court in her entire life. Today, she decided to watch this trial firsthand, so she could be better prepared in case one of her readers wrote her a question about the outcome. She noticed several of her female acquaintances sitting around the room. Clytee waved her fingers toward each, smiled, and mouthed a "Hello!" Then she turned to the activity. She noticed the bikers on the two front rows. Her eyes went to the lovely court reporter, who smiled in acknowledgement, as her busy fingers moved over the stenotype.

Clytee became aware that the biker who was on trial was staring intently at her. He gave her a huge smile, several exaggerated winks, and furiously wiggled the tip of his tongue at her. Clytee tittered! She was feeling young again.

Suddenly, Stanley heard an explosion behind him. The trial stopped. All heads in the room turned to the source of the noise. Clytee had discovered the TV set and reacted by standing up and shrieking at the judge. She ignored where she was and shouted, "What in the hell is going on in here? This is the most ridiculous event I've ever witnessed. Of all things, having a baseball game on while y'all are trying to send this nice, handsome man to the pen."

She proceeded to lambaste the jurors, causing them to duck their heads. Then she turned to the judge, "Bill Haller, I'm ashamed of you. I watched you grow up here in Cade County. I never thought you, of all people, would allow a travesty such as this to go on."

Clytee wouldn't shut up. "I changed your diapers when you were a baby. Your willy should be bigger than it was then. But from what I hear your wife is telling around town, it's ....."

"Chambers! Chambers!" Judge Haller shouted as he fled the bench, his black robe flaring out like bat wings.

The lawyers, clerk, and court reporter followed him into his office. Red-faced, he instructed, "I'm declaring a mistrial."

Turning to the district attorney, he said, "If you want to prosecute that biker again, get another judge. I'll have to leave town for a while until this dies down. I don't need to be a subject of Clytee's column."

DRIVER'S FLAT

The district attorney turned to the public defender and explained, "I'm dropping the charges against him for vandalizing the kiosks at the Sonic last year because they got his order mixed up and gave him a strawberry milkshake instead of banana! My witnesses would probably be intimidated, anyway, by all his rough buddies sitting in the courtroom."

No one objected.

Judge Haller ruefully admitted, "I know that I shouldn't have had the ball game on. With the playoffs coinciding with my October term of court, I would never have been able to summons enough jurors for trials. Most men in the county grew up as Cardinal fans."

Stanley watched the excitement in the courtroom ebb and flow. Clytee was the immediate center of attention. All of her lady friends rushed over and congratulated her for having the courage to confront Judge Haller. Clytee was informed that every October he twisted the arm of a local appliance dealer to place a TV in the courtroom so the jurors could watch the games.

A bailiff edged up and confided, "It's about time someone got on to him about his behavior!"

"Oh, is there something else?" asked Clytee.

"Yes! During testimony at trials, he routinely lets lawyers parade into the courtroom and approach the bench with an order to be signed. Regardless that it causes a distraction to the matter at hand."

"What's his excuse for that?"

"Oh, he claims his workload is so heavy he is forced to squeeze in all the cases he can. He blames the legislature for not adding another judge to the district."

One of the assistant clerks, a tall, sharply dressed young man chimed in, "And let me tell you how many times he has dozed off on the bench after lunch in the middle of a trial!"

The bailiff revealed, "Yeah. One time during a nap, a lawyer objected to what a witness was saying. The opposite counsel rebutted. They went at it, back and forth, while glancing at the sleeping judge."

"What happened?" asked Clytee.

"Oh, the other lawyer sat down without a ruling on the objection, and the questions continued."

Stanley snorted. He guessed that objections must have little value in these country courts. He would need to form a strategy to keep this unpredictable judge from presiding over the McCord case.

The courtroom emptied. The circuit clerk was the only one who noticed that Loophole never showed to present his motion, effectively abandoning his effort to quash Shifty's indictment.

CHAPTER 32
OFFICE CONFERENCE

Loophole was making last-minute preparations for the upcoming Shifty McCord trial. It was a difficult case, so he asked Archie Baker to assist. Archie had reluctantly agreed because he expected Shifty to be convicted. He didn't like to get beat, especially in a trial that would be highly publicized because of the large number of plants that had been seized.

Archie and Larry discussed trial tactics. Archie would handle the jury selection, or *voir dire*, and would make the opening statement. Thereafter, Loophole would cross-examine the prosecutor's witnesses. Archie would manage their checklist of evidence that had to be proven by the prosecution and would observe all pertinent courtroom activity.

The defense lawyers had been having trouble explaining to their client what was to be expected, how each trial aspect was to be addressed, and having him fully understand. Shifty was bull-headed. He insisted on testifying. He truly believed that he was slick enough to talk his way out of this mess. He said, "All I have to do is get up and repeat my campaign slogan, 'I'm just a farmer.' Nobody is going to send a hard-working man to jail over a few acres of weed. Especially if you tell them on the front-end what my defense is."

DRIVER'S FLAT

Archie rolled his eyes. "Sure, Shifty. I'm going to drive that point home in my opening statement to the jury. Just as you say."

Shifty shook with laughter. "I'm going to be there early. I hear there will be a big crowd. I need to circulate and thank everybody who voted for me for sheriff a few weeks ago."

Loophole scolded him, "That won't be possible because you'll be in leg irons until you're seated at our table."

Shifty countered, "Well, just before the judge comes in, I'll stand up and make a speech. I'll have it done before anybody stops me!"

Both lawyers scowled. Loophole's role in representing Shifty was getting off to a rocky start.

Defense attorney Archie was disturbed that the Memphis law firm of Janes, Knobly, and Stilt had intervened and was to aid the prosecution. Archie had already faced off with the firm in the will contest; Archie knew its lawyers were good, but abrasive, in the courtroom. He was unduly curious why Shifty's case had attracted a private prosecutor. Usually, a victim's family hired assistance to facilitate a conviction. There was no obvious victim in this case. This smelled like Shifty had stiffed someone who was seeking vengeance.

The Memphis firm, after hearing of Clytee's antics, promptly moved for Judge Haller to recuse himself from Shifty's upcoming trial. He gladly did.

Archie had become very angry when he heard about Clytee's scene in the courtroom at the biker trial, which gave the judge a reason to recuse himself. Showing the playoff games during October court terms was an annual ritual, and no one had ever complained. He had counted on Judge Haller presiding over Shifty's trial. Archie had been in his court many

DRIVER'S FLAT

times and knew what to expect from the bench. Haller also turned a blind eye to Archie's usual antics.

Archie was further disturbed when a few days earlier, the state attorney general had called and informed them that his office was taking over the prosecution of the trial; the local district attorney would still be involved, but from a backseat. It was rumored that Mississippi Attorney General Tom Turner would be running for U. S. Senator next year. Loophole and Archie concluded that he needed the limelight for a leg-up in the future race. They were told that his best trial team would be prosecuting Shifty.

Nevertheless, these interventions did made Archie eager for the trial. He thrived on facing heavyweights. The more, the better!

Then the Chief Justice of the State Supreme Court called and announced that he had appointed a retired judge on senior status to preside over the trial in place of Judge Haller. Loophole was horrified when told the judge was Pauline Brister. Judge Brister was from the Mississippi coast and had a reputation of being a warhorse. Although Loophole had not been in her court, he was wary of her. After retirement, Judge Brister filled in around the state when judges had conflicts. She was old-school and a stickler about lawyers' pleadings as to punctuation and as to correctness of their context. She was not bashful about berating lawyers in front of their clients. She ran her courtroom with the same approach as that of an army drill sergeant. Sternly.

All the coast lawyers detested her. Presenting a routine order for her signature was not a simple task. She read every word in the pleading and would rearrange words or phrases with a heavy red or purple ink pen. Then she might ask the unlucky lawyer to explain the underlying law of the issues used to support the request. Since there were two other judges in her district, the local lawyers began to dodge her by driving many miles to see another judge. Judge Brister began to notice the courtroom would be empty on her day to preside which caused her to mandate that none of the other judges could sign an order for a case already assigned to her by the computer.

Bespectacled Pauline was a striking figure. She had grey hair, and her dress was impeccable and fashionable. Prior to entering the legal profession, she had taught English at Ocean Springs High for ten years. She had been so strict in her classes that her departure was met with glee from the students and faculty alike.

Loophole had filed a pre-trial motion to suppress the search warrant used by the law to raid Shifty's farm. He had discovered several weak points and believed he could get it thrown out. Then he could get Shifty off because the prosecutor would have an empty case. When he called Judge Brister's administrative assistant to get a hearing date, he was informed that Judge Brister didn't do motions until after the trial started. Judge Brister expected the lawyers to argue all motions at the appropriate point during testimony. He was also warned that Judge Brister didn't play around with frivolous motions, allowed no nonsense, and detested any gambits that would cause a mistrial.

Loophole relayed the conversation to Archie who replied, "I think for one time in your life, you should knot your tie properly because I can foresee you disobeying that judge!"

Loophole lit a cigarette, wobbled his head and muttered, "Damn if that's so! I do things my way. Especially in my own briar patch. The courtroom is my favorite den of iniquity."

DRIVER'S FLAT

CHAPTER 33
THE TRIAL (PHASE I)

The courtroom was packed two hours before Shifty's trial started. The front rows behind the rail on one side of the courtroom were reserved for the press. The entire other side was filled by potential jurors. Because of the publicity of the drug bust, the district attorney had wisely advised that extra jurors be summoned. The walls were lined two-deep with spectators. Excitement abounded. Most of those in the courtroom knew Shifty and were eager to see how he would manage to squirm out of his current mess. They had learned that Archie and Loophole were defending Shifty; and that the state attorney general's office would lead the prosecution, aided by a prestigious Memphis law firm. They expected to be entertained by this array of big wheels.

The spectators were sizing up the individuals in the jury pool. They began to discuss which way they thought each would vote, even before any evidence was presented by the prosecution. They also talked about how they would vote, based on rumors and coffee shop talk. Opinions flowed freely.

Among the spectators was Jon David Knox who said, "Whether Shifty is guilty or not, I don't think the attorney general should be sticking his nose in our business up here."

DRIVER'S FLAT

Another agreed, "Yeah. Shifty hadn't sold any of the weed. No harm was done!"

A third added, "He's already suffered enough. The law tore down all his cotton and soybeans getting those marijuana plants out. That might cause him to lose his old family land."

The room became silent as a door opened and a short, heavy-set man entered, pulling a luggage cart stacked with recording equipment. All eyes were on him. Oblivious to his audience, he proceeded to arrange the devices on the court reporter's table. Al Bowers was an older man and was wearing a bow tie, pink shirt, pleated charcoal trousers, and black-and-white saddle oxford shoes. The eye-catcher of his dress was his black suspenders, decorated with yellow smiley faces. His dark hair was parted in the middle. As he struggled to remove all his gear, he contorted his round face with expressions, ranging from disgust to irritation to contentment, all to the amusement of the local eyes.

Shortly after, a group of lawyers, dressed in black suits and led by the local district attorney, entered. They set up shop at the table in front of the jury box. A few minutes later, a different set of lawyers joined them. These were from the Memphis firm that was assisting in the prosecution of Shifty. Senior Partner Povall Janes introduced Stanley Robbs, Lillie Bess Dorgan, and Rusty Stilt to the prosecutors. Povall had already met with the state's team to agree on a plan to successfully prosecute Shifty. Lillie Bess, a former beauty queen, was wearing a simple black sheath dress with matching cloth belt. Povall and Rusty had dressed down, but Stanley was wearing an expensive tailored suit, a floral Hermes pocket square, a hand-made tie, and Testoni alligator shoes.

Povall had been shocked when he saw Stanley's appearance before they left Memphis. He pointed out that a rural jury might view him as being condescending, which could cause them to sympathize with the farmer defendant.

DRIVER'S FLAT

"It's important to our client that Mr. McCord gets put away. We're out-of-towners, anyway, and need all the help we can get. Why don't we run by your house on the way out and you can change?"

Stanley had refused. "McCord is a dead duck. There's no way he can avoid jail. This is a slam-dunk case. I'm gonna show those clodhoppers how things are done in the big city!" crowed Stanley.

Lillie Bess had replied, "Yeah, just like you did when we went down there last year and lost that will contest."

Stanley's face reddened, but he still refused to change clothes.

Archie Baker strutted in, followed by Loophole. They placed their cases on the opposite table, next to the clerk's space. Archie was neatly dressed, but Loophole had on a white shirt with visible cigarette burns, a stained blazer with frayed sleeves, and scruffy penny loafers.

Archie glanced toward the other lawyers. Each was intently focused on the screen of his or her computer. When he caught Stanley's eye, he gave him a vigorous bent-elbow, closed fist upward gesture. The crowd exploded with mirth!

Many knew how Archie had trounced Stanley in this same courtroom only a year earlier.

Stanley jumped up so quickly his chair clattered back onto the floor. He yelled, "Why, you slimeball! I'll whip your ..."

He trailed off when the door to the judge's chambers opened. The bailiff commanded, "All rise. The Circuit Court of Cade County, Mississippi, is now in session. Mrs. Pauline Brister presiding. Be seated."

Judge Brister sternly scolded the bailiff, "Mr. Bailiff, your announcement was incorrect. I'm Senior Judge Pauline Brister. Not a 'Mrs.' That is a sexist remark."

"Oh." replied the perplexed bailiff, the circuit clerk's nephew who barely finished the seventh grade. He turned to the courtroom and ordered, "All re-rise." Everyone did, including the judge. He continued, "You all know where you are and this place is being run by Senior! Judge! Pauline Brister!" He wailed the last four words loudly. The lawyers sniggered silently.

The judge proceeded to lay down ground rules about how the trial would be conducted and what behavior she expected from the lawyers, jury, clerks, and spectators. Looking directly at Loophole, she said, "There also will be no smoking in this courtroom or in the halls."

Then she addressed the jury pool: "I will ask you potential jurors certain questions. Afterwards, the lawyers for the prosecution and for the defense will also ask some. The whole purpose of this is to ensure that the twelve of you selected and the two alternates will be fair and impartial to both sides in reaching a verdict in this case."

She went through a series of questions about whether or not anyone was related to Shifty McCord, had a grudge against him, had business dealings with him, had sat on a jury in the past year, and so forth. A few were weeded out.

Then she asked, "Is any one of you an alcoholic?"

No response.

"Is any one of you a drug addict?"

No response.

"Does any one of you have a gambling problem?"

No response.

She was in the middle of her next question, when a young man in the middle of the jurors stood up and interrupted, "Judge, back on that question about an alcoholic. I drink a six-pack every Saturday night."

DRIVER'S FLAT

The crowd cackled! The judge beamed and said, "That's not so bad. You can stay; and this being a dry county, I won't ask you where the beer comes from."

Then the judge deferred to the prosecution. Stanley had been appointed to handle the selection, or *voir dire*. The goal was to eliminate any sympathizers for Shifty in the group. Stanley rose and walked to the rail.

He asked, "Do any of you smoke weed?"

Archie bounced to his feet to object, but the judge tapped the bench with her gavel. "Mr. Robbs, that question is not permitted. You're asking for a confession to a crime. Proceed," she ordered.

Stanley asked, "How many of you voted for Shifty McCord to be sheriff of this county?" While sitting in jail awaiting trial, Shifty had received 400 votes to the amazement of the electorate.

Before Archie could move to object, the judge scolded, "Mr. Robbs, voting is a privilege exercised in private. I will not allow that question. Proceed."

Stanley ended his *voir dire* without discovering any biased jurors.

Archie, aware of Loophole's knowledge of each juror's background, shrewdly stayed with low-key questions. He didn't want a question to cause a person to be identified as having sympathy for Shifty, thus giving the prosecution a reason to strike the juror. Loophole had not identified any obvious pro-law person on the jury list. The defense lawyers were hoping to get someone on the jury who would help hang the verdict.

After Archie sat down, the judge announced, "This trial will probably last all week. Does anyone here have an excuse that would prevent you serving on the jury? Work? Sick relatives? Doctors' appointments?" Silence.

Judge Brister called both sides into chambers for the jury selection. The lawyers filled all chairs, and some were standing against the walls.

The judge remarked to no one, "This is the first trial I've presided over that not a single person tried to get off serving on a jury. Can any of y'all explain that?"

There was some shuffling. Finally, the district attorney spoke, "This arrest made the national headlines because of the size of the bust, and, at the same time, Shifty was running for sheriff. Probably everyone out there sees an opportunity to be on the jury and enjoy a good bit more than 'fifteen minutes of fame.'"

Povall agreed, "Books and TV appearances could be in the wings."

Loophole scoffed, "I think it's because the county started paying $40 a day, plus travel, for jury fees."

Stanley Robbs blurted, "That's it. That's the most money most of these yokels will ever see in one day!"

Povall looked at the ceiling, rolled his eyes, and thought, "Why didn't I leave him in Memphis?"

Loophole remarked to the judge, "I live here. I'm offended by that remark! I think I'll just jack his jaw."

The judge spoke to Loophole, "Hold on now. I demand civility between the lawyers. And look at you two: one dressed like a popinjay and the other like a skid-row bum."

"Calling him a bum is an upgrade!" sneered Stanley.

She looked over her glasses at Loophole and spoke in a condescending manner, "*Vestis Virum Reddit.*"

She was taken aback when Loophole snarled, "*Et tu, Brute.*" She had assumed that Loophole was Latin-ignorant. His reply wasn't exactly on point, but she gave him mental credit.

Judge Brister ignored his response and continued, "Mr. Lawrence, your shoes look like they were shined with a

DRIVER'S FLAT

chocolate bar. Tomorrow, see if you can't get them to look better, or I'll make you knot your tie properly!"

Loophole didn't want that, so he meekly replied, "Yes, ma'am."

"It's 'Yes, Your Honor!'"

After sparring for a half-hour, the lawyers agreed to the twelve jurors and the two alternates.

The jury was seated: seven women and five men. A variety of ages, education, employment, and religion was represented by the twelve. Neither side had any inkling if it might have an edge.

Now that the jury had been selected, the local district attorney left the courtroom in disgust. His only role in the trial had ended.

An assistant attorney general made the opening statement for the prosecution. He pointed out they were going to prove, beyond a reasonable doubt, that Shifty knowingly planted 14,000 marijuana plants with the intent to harvest and distribute them in violation of the law.

He ended his speech by reminding the jurors, all of whom were registered voters, "When Mr. McCord qualified as a candidate for your sheriff's office, he made the statement that he would make the county a better place to live by keeping drugs OUT of the county, but all the while, he had acres of marijuana planted on his farm. In his own way, he was keeping the promise because he was shipping the weed away from here."

To his satisfaction, many of the jurors nodded in agreement.

Archie came next. He walked from one end of the jury box to the other, talking as he paced. To emphasize a point, he would wheel and face the jury with his back to the prosecutors.

175

He began to make outrageous remarks. "We're going to show you that Mr. Shifty McCord is innocent." He then gave the jury a wink. In the middle of the front row, an overweight pulpwood cutter dressed in faded blue overalls winked back.

"We'll show you that Mr. McCord is 'just a farmer,'" said Archie, and winked again. The pulpwooder winked back.

"We'll further show you that Mr. McCord, honestly and innocently, went to the local seed store and ordered bags of milo seeds to plant. The co-op made a mistake and sold Mr. McCord marijuana seeds!" said Archie, and delivered an exaggerated wink. This time, the pulpwooder mimicked the huge wink.

The spectators hooted at this revelation. The prosecutors rolled their eyes in disgust. The judge called the room to order. Stanley, who had seen the pulpwooder wink, popped to his feet and shouted, "What's going on here? Judge, this looks like home-cooking to me."

He told the judge what he had seen.

The judge addressed the juror, "Did you wink at Mr. Baker?"

The pulpwooder, realizing that he had been caught, and not wanting to come across as dumb as he looked, replied innocently, "Yes, Judge. But I've got painful hemorrhoids, which makes me squint from time to time, just to keep from yelling."

Attorney Lillie Bess Dogan put her head in her hands, thinking, "What a sideshow. It gets worse every time my firm shows up here."

The judge studied the juror. The school teacher in her came out, and without thinking, she addressed him seriously, "I can relate. You may be excused if you're uncomfortable."

The burly juror declined.

DRIVER'S FLAT

Archie made his last remark. As he spoke, he raised his voice and began to wave his arms wildly above his shoulders. Several of the female jurors frowned with concern. It appeared that he might soar away. "In law school, we were taught that if the other side comes to trial with apples, you need to come with oranges, or there is no need to be there. Mr. Lawrence and I are gonna turn the prosecution's wormy, dried-up apples into big, juicy, delicious oranges, and you will gladly release our client from his bondage to return to his honest profession of being 'just a farmer'!"

Groans were heard coming from the Memphis lawyers. The judge tittered, thinking that the nature of Archie's remarks indicated he knew he was facing a losing battle.

The first witness called by the prosecution was Lou Bertha Eason. She waddled to the bench and was sworn in by the court reporter, Al Bowers, who double-jiggled his eyebrows at her as she passed. She giggled and seated herself in the witness chair.

Stanley Robbs waited until she got comfortable. He proceeded to ask her the standard witness questions of her name, her age, where she lived, her means of making a living. Then he asked if she knew Shifty McCord.

Stanley asked, "Do you owe Mr. Shifty McCord anything?"

"No, I don't. But he owes me for fo' flats ..."

"Objection. That's irrelevant," said Archie.

"Sustained," said the judge. "This is not a debt case."

Stanley asked Lou Bertha, "Were you on Mr. McCord's property on the last Friday of this past August?"

"I sho was."

"Explain that day to the jury."

"Well, I had parked my car on the road against them woods where that big hill runs off into a cotton field."

DRIVER'S FLAT

"Why were you there?"

"I was scoutin' for muscadines to gather later to make my pies. I gots turned around, and 'stead of coming back to the road, I come out in a cotton field. That cotton was already waist high."

"Did you see anything unusual in the field?"

"I sho did. Down every row there was some high, green stalks about a yard apart. At first, I thought I was seein' polk salet. But it's too late in the year to gather that plant. So, I said to my self, 'Self, look over yonder at all that marijuana.'"

"Objection!" screamed Loophole as he scrambled out of his chair. "What one says to theirself is hearsay!"

Archie interjected, "No, it's not!"

The judge's jaw dropped. "Now, wait a minute. Am I hearing that one member of the defense team is objecting to the other's objection? That's preposterous."

"I can explain," said Archie.

"Please do," said Judge Brister. "And only one of you is to speak."

Archie cleared his throat, "What my colleague means is that when one testifies as to what they said to themselves, it's not hearsay, it's double hearsay!"

Stanley interrupted, "Oh, get real! Whoever heard of that? She can certainly voice her thoughts."

Archie replied, "But not in that manner. Judge, I move that the testimony of this witness be excluded. She's already got it in for Shifty because of the flats. If my motion is upheld, I move that the search warrant be suppressed because it's based on Lou Bertha's observations."

Judge Brister snickered. "Mr. Baker, is this a 'double' motion?"

Archie's face reddened and he sat down.

Before Stanley could get her stopped, Lou Bertha blurted from the witness chair, "And I gots somethin' else to say about

Shifty. When I come out of the field at the road, a wire was blockin' me. When I puts my hand down to push the wire lower so I could step over, blue flames shot six inches off my fingers and I wets my pants! That fool done put hot wires around his marijuana fields."

The spectators and the jury howled!

The judge announced that there would be a short recess so she could go to chambers and research the law for Archie's motion.

The judge returned and announced, "My ruling is that the witness appears to be biased, whether she heard what she said to herself, or not. Also, the prosecutor didn't lay the foundation of how Lou Bertha would know that the plants she saw were marijuana prior to her statement to that effect in open court. I'm ruling that the testimony of Lou Bertha Eason be stricken from the record, and the jury is not to consider her remarks. But I'm not throwing the search warrant out yet because it's also based on the testimony of the Webster County sheriff. I'm sure the prosecutor will let us hear what he has to say later."

Next, the youngest member of the prosecutor's team put on a crime lab expert from Jackson. The witness was asked questions that qualified him as an expert on marijuana evidence. The defense didn't object to any of them.

The young lawyer was obviously the most handsome of all seated at his table. He picked up a clear gallon bag of weed from a box on the floor. As he walked around the room asking questions of his witness, he waved the bag. The jurors' faces followed him, all staring at the bag. Loophole seethed. The prosecutor's actions were close to being objectionable. But he had not said a word about the bag's contents. There was nothing Loophole could do about the visible parade.

Archie zeroed in on one young woman on the front row of the jury. A few days ago, he had dropped by Potshot's Poolroom for a game of snooker. Spider Webb had sidled up to him and told about her being on the jury list and about her behavior at the roadblock at Shifty's land, and what she had said there. This juror was the one the prosecutors had tried to exclude from the jury, but their objections were too weak. Her name also ended up in a position on the list that was immune from their two automatic strikes from the top.

As the young prosecutor moved from the witness to the end of his table and back, Archie noticed the eyes of the female jurist intently following him. She turned her head, then her entire body, toward the young man as he moved, holding the bag in the air. Her eyes glazed. Her breathing noticeably increased. Her mouth opened, and Archie could see a pearl barbell in her pierced tongue! He nearly gagged. Saliva drooled from the corners of her mouth. "Man, is she that hot for the lawyer?" wondered Archie. Then the lawyer placed the bag of weed back into its box and walked to the witness. The woman's eyes stayed locked on the box. Archie exhaled and said to himself, "We've got a hung jury!"

After a series of witnesses testified to the details of the raid, the judge remarked, "That's enough for today. Jury selection caused a late start of the trial. We'll continue at eight tomorrow."

The next morning, more witnesses testified. All the objections made by the defense were overruled. Loophole and Archie were sinking lower into their seats. But Shifty didn't seem to be disturbed. He was certain he could get on the stand and win over the jury.

The next witness called by the prosecutor was Webster County Sheriff Marter. Calling him last was intentional. He would be the final shot the defense would have to suppress the search warrant. By now, even if they were successful, the jury would have heard all the damaging evidence against Shifty.

The lead assistant attorney general went over the events leading to the stop of the three youngsters in whose car the plants were found. Then he tendered the witness to the defense.

Loophole did the cross-examination. "How did you know horses were in the Caderetta Road?"

"I was making a routine patrol down the road and nearly hit one. Then, by the headlights of an oncoming car, I could see dozens milling against a pasture fence."

"Whose horses were they?"

"I don't know."

"Did you try to find out?"

"Nope."

"Why not?" Loophole asked.

"I went back out there the next morning, but I didn't see the horses. I got an urgent call and had to return to my office before I could do more."

"Did you see any horse tracks in the dirt road?"

"Oh, yeah. There were lots of them. Sort of all around in one area. Then they disappeared."

"Disappeared?"

The sheriff turned his head to one side to hide a grin and said, "Yeah. At one place, they were all in lines headed down the road. Then, no more tracks. Like they went airborne."

The judge snorted.

Stanley rose. "Now judge, I object to this line of questions. My witness has not been qualified to be an expert on horse tracks. For all we know, those impressions in the dirt could have been made by a group of migrating terrapins."

The judge said, "Sustained. I don't want to hear anymore about horse tracks."

Loophole waved his hands in disgust and said, "Okay. I'm through with this witness."

He had sent a friend, Little Ben Weaver, to find out if any horses had been loose on the road that night. Ben had bird hunted in that area and knew everyone in the community. He reported back that no one for miles along that road had horses in their pastures or had seen any in the road. Loophole knew that this horse charade had been made up by the sheriff to cover his unauthorized stop of those boys. And he knew that Sheriff Marter knew that he knew.

Sheriff Marter stepped down from the witness chair. The lead prosecutor stood and announced, "Your Honor, the State rests."

Archie and Loophole had a whispered conversation. All eyes in the courtroom were on them. Loophole pulled a certain paper from a stack and pored over it with Archie. Shifty was not involved. He was rehearsing in his mind what he was going to say when he was called as the first witness.

Archie stood and announced, "Your Honor, we have a motion for a mistrial."

The prosecutors were looking at each other blankly. None could recall even the slightest misstep on their part. The judge was frowning. She had not noticed one either.

Judge Brister looked at her watch. It was nearly noon. She said, "This will be heard after lunch." She asked sweetly, "Mr. Baker, will your motion involve any of your so-called oranges?"

Archie smacked a fist into an open palm and gleefully replied, "Only one, Your Honor. And it's going to be a blue-ribbon specimen. Grown right here in this very courtroom. And fertilized by my opposition!"

"Very well. I can't wait to hear your motion. Court is adjourned until two o'clock. I have to do some paperwork on the lunch hour. Everyone stay seated while the jury is escorted out."

The courtroom cleared. The judge entered her chambers with her notes. As she munched on a tuna sandwich, Archie's remarks stayed on her mind. What was he up to? Was he bluffing? She had noticed Loophole looking at the ceiling like he was about to enter Heaven.

Sheriff Grady Powers and Deputy Wade Sumrall headed back to their office. They had not missed a minute of the trial. Grady said, "I want Shifty convicted. He spread a lot of lies about me during the campaign. Hurt my wife's feelings."

"I'm worried," said Wade. "Archie and Loophole have detected something. I don't know what, but I'm saying this case is about to be thrown out."

"We don't need a mistrial. That means another trial will have to be scheduled and we'll have to house that loudmouth until then."

Wade thoughtfully replied, "I've got an idea of how to get rid of Shifty in case Archie wins his motion."

"What?"

Wade elaborated a plan.

Grady brightened, "That'll work just fine! I need to run that person down. Now!"

He quickly dialed a number in Oxford that he had on file.

Archie's behavior was also bothering the prosecutors. Over a lengthy lunch, they rehashed the testimony of all the witnesses among themselves. They finally concluded their case was perfect.

As the team was entering the courthouse, two of the lawyers recognized several men in a small group standing at the far end of the hall. The assistant attorney general puzzled, "What's the U.S. Attorney and those marshals doing here?"

"I dunno," replied Rusty Stilt. "Maybe they just want to pick up some pointers from us."

CHAPTER 34
THE TRIAL (PHASE II)

As Loophole and Archie walked into the hall at the front entrance of the courthouse after lunch, they ran into Red, the gambler. "Why aren't you inside already?" asked Loophole.

Red grinned. "I lost my spot when I went to lunch. A lot of folks inside just skipped eating to hold their seats. The courtroom is buzzing about what Archie is going to say."

Judge Brister opened court, "You're on, Mr. Baker. Please be civil and get to the point. I don't want this court's time to be wasted."

Archie dawdled. He slowly circled the prosecution's table with his head down and his fingers laced behind his back. He came back to his table and shuffled through a stack of papers, searching.

The judge impatiently asked, "Do you need help, Mr. Baker?"

Stanley sneered, "He needs counseling!"

Archie jerked one page out and beamed. "Here it is! The answer!"

Behind the bailiff's back, the door to the jury room cracked open. By law, the jurors were not permitted to be in the courtroom while a motion was being heard. Faces could be seen peeping out. They all waited, including the bailiff, to hear Archie.

"Your Honor, first, I have a question."

"Go ahead."

"Before lunch, the prosecution rested their case. Does that mean that they can't call any more witnesses?"

Judge Brister sniped, "That's law school 101!"

"Your Honor, for the record, I need a 'Yes' or 'No' answer."

Al Bowers, the court reporter, tilted his head back and rolled it in circles, to the amusement of the crowd.

The judge rose and screamed at Archie, "It's NO! For the record that's spelled capital 'N', capital 'O'!"

Al's pencil snapped in two as he took down the remark.

"Your Honor," continued Archie, "does that mean that they are through?"

"YES!"

"And when you rule favorably on my motion, will the prosecutors have to say 'uncle' in open court?"

"Mr. Baker, I'm about done with you. Your arrogant attitude is causing me to think my ruling will be negative toward your client. And I demand you apologize!"

Archie meekly replied, "Why, sure. I apologize to the court. I got caught up and didn't realize I bumped one of your hot buttons."

Judge Brister stood up from her chair, pointed a finger at Archie and shrieked, "I don't have hot buttons. Don't you be talking about my body, young man."

Not a single sound was emitted from the courtroom. She continued, "I warn you. You better plead your motion here and now. The jail is too far away for your voice to be heard!"

Loophole was silently begging, "Shut up, man. You've pushed the envelope to its edge! We've got this won. Don't blow it!"

DRIVER'S FLAT

Archie began to flap his arms as he argued, "Your Honor, the prosecution has unnecessarily wasted the last few days presenting their bogus case. They have presented one witness after the other before the court to tell their stories."

He then proceeded to name each witness and gave a brief summary of what they had said. He ran through the names of each prosecutor involved.

"Your Honor, this case turns not on what was done but what wasn't done."

The prosecutors began to squirm, a few scraping their chairs on the floor.

At that moment everyone's attention was directed to Loophole, who made a stack of law books in the middle of his table. Loophole pulled a large navel orange from a bag underneath the table and placed it on the top book.

The judge gaveled the laughing spectators to order.

Lillie Bess wondered apprehensively if a navel orange had ever been used anywhere else in lieu of a drum roll.

Archie, with a smug grin, stated, "Your Honor, not a single witness presented by the prosecution has testified that the crime charged against Shifty McCord was committed yesterday, today, or tomorrow in Cade County, State of Mississippi, as the law requires. Therefore, I move for a mistrial!"

All the prosecutors rose, chorusing, "We object, Your Honor. That's a false claim!"

The judge began to go through her notes. She came to a typed checklist she had made of what had to be proven by the State to get Shifty convicted. She noticed one box hadn't been checked. She mentally cursed! Unbelievable! She thought, "Too many egotistical chiefs. They had forgotten to coordinate."

Judge Brister looked around the courtroom for several minutes. She didn't notice that Loophole had lit a cigarette, put his feet on the table, and was blowing a never-ending string of smoke rings upwards.

Finally, she spoke, "Gentlemen, I'm afraid he's correct. I will rule…"

"Now, wait a minute, Judge," Povall spoke urgently, as he glared at his team. "I know that SOMEONE covered that point. We need to have the court reporter read back all the testimony to double-check."

Al, the court reporter, with his bow tie dangling from his collar, mouthed a string of cuss words that was understood by the entire courtroom.

"That's not necessary, Mr. Povall. I routinely make a checklist of all matters that are to be proven for a trial to proceed. Your team failed to …"

Povall, the most experienced trial lawyer in the room, desperately resorted to a backdoor tactic: "Your Honor, as we all remember, several witnesses testified that those weed fields adjoined Shutispear Creek. And Shutispear Creek runs through Cade County. Therefore, Mr. Baker's motion should be overruled."

Loophole stood and countered, "Your Honor, Mr. Povall, not being from this area, doesn't realize that Shutispear Creek heads up in another county. I can bring in a witness …"

"No need to, Mr. Lawrence, I taught fifth grade geography when I did my practice teaching at Baxter. I know that the creek is located in more than one county. I take judicial notice of that fact and declare a mistrial."

She left the bench as the courtroom emptied. Shifty shook his lawyers' hands and said, "I'm going out to my truck and pass out Crown Royal to all my friends. I'm a free man!"

Loophole pointed out that the state could retry him and probably would.

DRIVER'S FLAT

Shifty laughed as he walked out the door. "I'm not worried. Those guys got beat so bad they won't mess with me again," he bragged.

A loud commotion was heard from the hall. Archie went out to see Shifty being put in handcuffs and leg irons by a federal marshal. The U.S. Attorney read Shifty his rights. He spoke to the onlookers, "The crime of growing marijuana can be prosecuted in federal or state courts. Shifty's next trial will be in my court in Oxford, and I won't forget where his fields are."

Stanley led the Memphis lawyers to their car. Povall was already calling his New Orleans clients. He would need to blame the mistrial on the state lawyers. His only "out" was that Shifty would be tried again in federal court, where a conviction would be a slam-dunk. The current U.S. Attorney had yet to lose a criminal trial.

As Stanley opened his car door, he let out words that would make a sailor blush. Oranges began rolling off the back seat onto the ground. Lots of them!

DRIVER'S FLAT

CHAPTER 35
THE "WASH"

Grady dropped by Wade's house on the Saturday morning after Shifty's arrest by the Feds. Grady's wife had baked a pecan pie and made some pimento cheese sandwiches with onion and hot peppers, especially for Wade.

Wade was sitting on an overturned bucket under his oak shade tree, peeling a bushel of pears. Grady grabbed a Diet Dr. Pepper from a nearby cooler and sat on his heels, leaning against the tree trunk. He liked to sit this way because he could rub his itches against the rough bark.

As Grady watched Wade at his task, he said, "I've been wondering about Primer's story. I'm worried about those guys at the campfire. Their description makes them seem like hard cases. Hiding in a tree as a sentry and using tracers."

Wade replied, "Yeah, my thoughts exactly. And the deal about the pickup being bumped by a ghost vehicle."

"Think back. That banker's wife referred to something similar. And she didn't see a vehicle leaving the scene after their car hit the water."

"I wonder if the two incidents are connected?"

Grady added, "Another thing that's worrying me... that tip came in from the Alabama real estate magnate about finding the dumped dog food in the woods. We were able to follow tractor tracks off Shifty's land to the gravel road. On down the road a piece, they turned onto the road Mr. Shaw told us about."

Wade noted, "Between the time he found the dump and called in the tip, a load of cereal had been added to the pile."

"What's really bothering me is where did Shifty get 14,000 seeds to plant marijuana?" asked Grady.

"Either he had enough of a grow the past year to save the seeds to plant or someone else is furnishing them."

"I'll go for that last part. He had to already have a market to ship the harvested weed. You can't peddle that much around here and not get caught. Somebody would tell. There is always a rat in Cade County."

Wade agreed. "Well, that's in the Feds hands now. Thank goodness. They have the resources to find whoever is up the line."

On Tuesday, Fred Roberts, the FBI agent, called Sheriff Powers. "We just got a call from that tenacious lawyer in Pontotoc, Phil Blackstone. He is representing L.C. Sykes, who you are holding. Sykes appears to be Shifty's foreman. He wants to cut a deal."

"Oh?"

"Yes. According to the lawyer, he can tell us about an operation bigger than those weed fields. And he wants witness protection."

"Wow!"

"It'll have to be large for the U.S. Attorney to grant that request. Can we meet with your staff tomorrow afternoon?"

"Sure thing."

Shortly after 1:00, Fred, two U.S. Marshals, a stenographer, Deputy Sumrall, Sheriff Powers, the summer deputies, and lawyer Phil Blackstone were seated around the conference room. The door opened and Deputy Baker led L.C. Sykes to a chair in the room. L. C. was a lanky, gray-haired man. He was nervously rubbing his hands on his trousers.

"This proceeding is off the record. If you don't offer L.C. the deal he wants, he will take his chances at trial. Agreed?" spoke Phil.

Fred replied, "If we can verify what he tells us, it's a deal."

"He wants witness protection in exchange for his testimony."

"That's an extreme request."

L. C. burst into the conversation, "No, it ain't, if you're gonna get killed for what you know!"

The young deputies gawked at him. All three had grown up in the same community with L.C. and had a soft spot for the older man. The boys used to give him money to go into the country store and buy their chewing tobacco. If they bought the tobacco themselves, the old storekeeper might tell their parents. They didn't want him to get hurt. L.C. had worked on Shifty's farm most of his adult life. He was a hard worker and didn't waste his paycheck. He had a community reputation of being loyal to Shifty.

"Tell these lawmen what you know," instructed Phil.

"Shifty was buyin' overruns and seconds of dog food from a factory in Louisville, and he was sellin' some at discount prices to stores 'round here. But he was dumping most of the feed in the middle of the woods over by Bethel Church and fillin' the empty sacks with weed. He been doin' that fo three years; his operation be bigger each year. He was sendin' the sacks of weed to a warehouse in New Orleans along with empty cereal boxes that he was getting from a container factory south of here. The folks in New Orleans would fill the cereal boxes with money and truck them back to Shifty's farm." L. C. continued to rub his hands on his pants. He rocked back and forth while sitting on the edge of the chair.

He went on with his story. "There, me and Shifty would fill the cargo van with seed corn over the cereal boxes. The driver would then take it to some place over on the Mississippi River where it would be loaded on a barge with other vans of grain. Shifty said stolen or counterfeit custom seals would be put on the van. The barge would carry its load to the Intracoastal Waterway and on to a port to be loaded on a freighter. The cargo vans would never be checked again after the seal was placed on them."

"Was a load of corn and money ever intercepted?" asked Fred.

L.C. replied, "No. They had a clever operation."

"Then why are you scared?"

"A while back, a shipment of money disappeared between New Orleans and Cade County. The man in New Orleans alerted Shifty that he shouldn't expect the truck and trailer. Shifty already knew that because he's the one who stole it!"

"How did he succeed in the heist?"

"The same driver would bring the money each time. Shifty would carry on a bunch of his usual bull, and the driver got to be buddies with him. Shifty found out that the driver had a weakness for whiskey and 'lot lizards'. They's a rest stop on I-55, just south of Gallatin, that is regularly worked by local women, mostly skanks." L. C. stopped and looked at the officers. He wondered if they believed him.

L.C. told them that Shifty arranged for two strippers from a club in Memphis to make contact with the driver at the rest stop on his next trip. "It was nearly midnight when the driver pulled into the rest stop and parked. Me and Shifty were in an old dump truck a few parking slots over. The two girls got out of their van and walked to the truck. Man! You shoulda seen them. They both looked better than that woman who blocks driveways at the sausage factory!"

"Huh?" puzzled Fred.

The young deputies laughed, and Spider wised off, "Pamela Anderson! You must live a sheltered life."

Red-faced, Fred asked L. C., "What happened then?"

"Normally, the skank gets into the cab with a trucker. But the girls didn't have any trouble getting the driver to join them in their van. He left his engine running and followed them like a little puppy dog. We waited until the party started. Shifty sneaked up to the truck, got into the cab, and drove off."

"Where did he go?"

"He knew the area, so he drove it down a nearby remote dirt road with me following in the dump truck. There, me and him transferred the boxes to the dump truck. While we were working, Shifty was belly-laughing so hard he was shaking and saying, 'This is easier than taking candy from a baby!'

"Shifty ran the empty, stolen rig deep into the surrounding woods. We broke off pine limbs and wiped out the tire tracks in the dust. Then we took backroads through Montgomery County going home."

"What did Shifty do with the money?" asked Fred.

L.C. said, "Shifty figured that he would be checked out since the semi-truck was stolen so close to his farm. He hid it where they wouldn't look. In plain sight." L.C. looked over his shoulder toward the door.

"So, the next day, Shifty took one full cereal box out and drove the dump truck over to my grandpa's place, about ten miles from Shifty's farm. We parked that old dump truck full of money in an open shed. You can see the truck from the road," he explained.

"We left the hood raised after Shifty pulled the coil wire off. I took a front wheel off and left the jack underneath so

DRIVER'S FLAT

folks would think it was broke down. No telling how many people drove by without knowing they were close to a fortune!"

Phil Blackstone spoke, "Shifty was afraid that the currency might be compromised. The money had to be coming from all directions into New Orleans. It could be marked or contain drug residue. He wanted to trade the cash for new bills. His cousin, Craig Synott, from over in Lodi, just happened to be the manager of the Driver's Flat bank. The two devised a plan to make the exchange. Since Shifty knew he could be watched for a while after the highjacking, he would have L.C. drive a load of cereal boxes to his cousin's bank."

The lawyer explained, "L.C. had a van. Shifty came up with a magnetized sign to put on the side: York's Cleaning Service. L.C. would drive behind the bank after the clerks had gone home. He and the cousin would take the load into the back door. Shifty had discovered that the dealer in New Orleans had a sheet in each cereal box with the money count. Later, Synott would substitute his bank documents with the same count after skimming his agreed share. He would put the cash in bank bags and trash the boxes. He would order a similar amount of money from a corresponding bank in new bills under the pretense they were needed for his ATM. There were several deliveries because the banker could only handle so much money at one time because of the bank's small size.

"The armored car would bring the new bills and pick up the drug money as excess cash held by the bank. Through a series of accounting entries, the swap would be covered, which amounted to a 'wash.'"

The men and the stenographer stared at Blackstone as he relayed what L. C. had told him.

"L.C. would go back on the next Saturday or Sunday in his 'cleaning' van, pick up the new bills, and store them in the dump truck bed," Phil Blackstone concluded.

DRIVER'S FLAT

"How would the banker have enough new money left for his ATM machine?" asked Sheriff Grady Powers.

"We've found out the bank's ATM activity was low. So, we figured he over-ordered enough money to meet that need."

"So that new money the robbers took was earmarked for Shifty?" asked Grady.

"Yes. L.C. said when he made his usual run on that Tuesday, just before Christmas, the banker told him he was leaving the next morning with his wife to spend a few days in Jackson to shop. The armored car would leave its shipment, but he didn't have time to bag the drug money. It would have to stay in a locked closet in the vault until next time," said Phil.

"Wow! Was that money still in the closet after the robbery?"

Fred, the FBI agent, interjected, "No. The closet was empty."

Grady whistled. "So the robbers got a two-for-one?"

"Yeah. But they had to know that the money wasn't extra cash for the bank's operations," added Fred.

"Can Shifty's money be located?" asked the sheriff.

Fred turned to L.C., "Can you take us to that old dump truck? That's part of the deal."

"I sho can," said L.C. "But all of the new money is gone. Shifty started taking it away somewhere right after some of it came up missing."

"Tell us about that."

"One day, when me and Shifty went to load another shipment for the bank, he noticed an empty money wrapper on the ground. They's supposed to be $10,000 in it. Another wrapper was beside that one with a single $100 bill still inside. He started cussing. After that, I noticed the rest of the new money was moved."

Deputy Wade Sumrall spoke, "That sure is odd. Someone taking $19,900 and not bothering the rest?"

DRIVER'S FLAT

"That's what I asked Shifty. He muttered something about payback. He said he knew who got it."

Wade frowned and asked, "When did that happen?"

"Late last summer."

"Is any of that drug money still in the truck?" asked Fred.

"Some. After the banker died, we couldn't take no mo up there. Shifty was trying to figure how to get rid of what's left."

Fred asked, "L.C., what makes you think there's a hit out on you?"

"A few days before the bust, I left my house to go to the farm sheds. I had got down the road from the house a piece when this cottonmouth came out from under my pickup seat. I bailed out of the truck with it still in gear and let it run on down the road. The truck nosed over into the grader ditch and stopped. I saw the snake slither out. It was a while before I could make myself get back in."

Wade smiled. "Was it a big snake?"

"It sho was! But not near as big as the one that came out of my mailbox. After I got home from work, I opened the lid to get my letters, and it struck at my arm. Lawdy, what a day! And there's more."

With concern, Fred asked, "What? More snakes?"

"Worse! The next morning, I was leaving the house at daylight and found my driveway blocked by a pickup. There was two masked men inside. The driver got out and asked, 'Are you L.C. Sykes?'"

"When I said I was, he shoved a big piece of cardboard through my open window. He started laughing, and I could hear the other one laughing louder. What I saw on the cardboard scared the bejesus out of me!"

Everyone in the room waited in suspense.

"Go on," urged Deputy Baker.

"It was drawed on like a tombstone. It had my name and birth date on it. But in the space for the death date was the words, 'To be filled in soon!'"

He continued, "Then the man said, 'See you later. We've got to go to the flower shop in Houston and buy a nice spray for your casket!'"

"Who were these men?"

"I dunno. I never seed them before. I was scaid."

"Would you recognize them again?"

"No. I was too scaid and the sky wasn't too bright."

"Do you still have the cardboard marker?" asked Deputy Baker.

L. C. exclaimed, "No way! I called ole Aunt Corrie, my neighbor down the road, for help. She shuffled up with a hoe in her one hand to fend off the haints, and a witches' bottle full of nail clippings and chicken blood in the other. I built a fire. She poured some drops of blood on each side of the cardboard. When it dried, she cast a 'woo-woo' on the sign and threw it into the flames!"

"What about the pickup? Did you see the tag?"

"They took off fast after he handed me my tombstone. The tag was covered with mud. The pickup was black and had a cattle pusher on the front bumper. Oh, yeah. It didn't make no noise going down the road."

He stopped and then added in a whisper, "Like a ghost."

Deputy Sumrall asked, "L.C., what happened to that one cereal box of money Shifty took out of the dump truck?"

L. C. frowned. "It came up missing. Shifty was going to use it for running money for his local expenses. The only thing we could figure was that those Mexican helpers got it mixed in with one of our dog food deliveries to the stores."

DRIVER'S FLAT

Fred left the room to call the U.S. Attorney, Bob Tate. He gave him the details of L.C.'s disclosures, and asked, "Is his confession and fear of a reprisal enough for witness protection?"

Bob thoughtfully replied, "Yes. At least we'll have the money that was in the hijacked truck to chase back down the line."

"I agree. Hopefully, we can trace it."

"We'll send him to a high-rise in Chicago," chuckled Bob. "Since he grew up in the country, he won't like that. In a couple of years, he'll bail out of the program. That'll save taxpayer money. By then, the mob will have settled with Shifty, one way or the other."

Fred came back and reported, "Bob agreed to witness protection. L.C., you should be safe now."

L.C. relaxed. "I want to go to them Cayman Islands I been seeing on the T.V., and waste the rest of my life dranking beer on the beach."

Fred scolded, "L.C., this is not like checking into a Holiday Inn. You're probably going to get an apartment in a high-rise building in Chicago."

L.C. groaned.

The meeting ended with Fred thinking that L.C. was safe, for the time being, from the two strangers.

"I think they suspected that Shifty was the one who had heisted the truck," said Fred.

"They were about to come down hard on L.C. to squeal."

"The raid nixed that," said Grady. "Now, they won't know where to look."

DRIVER'S FLAT

CHAPTER 36
THE NUMBERS

Tony had returned from his cross-country trip in his Kenworth truck. He dropped in at Lola's to catch up on the gossip. There he was told about Marvin's death. That news hit him hard, for he had given Marvin many free rides in the past. Marvin talked a lot and had entertained him with interesting stories about his travels.

When Little Ben told all about the accident, Tony exclaimed, "Dang! Rickey and I dodged it. But we didn't see Marvin. We would have stopped if we had known."

After a while, the others left and Tony ended up being alone at the table. He stared at his coffee, reminiscing about Marvin: his mandolin; his worn leather shoulder bag; his clothes, stylish for a hitchhiker; his colorful, trademark hat.

Hat? Tony ran out to his truck where the hat from his grille was still on the floorboard. He was standing by the open cab door holding the hat in his hand when Henry the Musician drove up.

The Musician recognized the hat, for he had given Marvin rides. He asked Tony, "What are you doing with Marvin Fant's hat?"

Tony explained how he and Rickey had sped past the accident scene where Marvin was killed. "I guess the hat flew into my grille and was lodged. Reckon what I ought to do with it?"

"Let me see it," said Henry. He took the hat and carefully examined it as Tony watched.

It wasn't damaged. The sweatband was slightly soiled. Henry peeled the band back and discovered a small, folded square of stiff paper. Inside the oily folds were no words, but there was a set of numbers. It had nine digits. Underneath it was a double number: 15.

Tony asked, "What do those numbers mean?"

"I dunno."

Henry's heart rate increased. He, along with everybody else, knew about Marvin's reputation for being rich, and he knew what the numbers meant.

He told Tony, "It looks like a bank number and maybe a lockbox number."

"Wow! If something of value is in that box and we could find it before Marvin's heirs do, we could get a finder's fee!"

"Boy, you wasn't born yesterday," noted Henry.

"Common sense runs in my family," mocked Tony.

Henry offered, "I know my way around. Let me see what I can come up with."

They agreed to a split of any reward on a handshake - with five percent to Tony.

DRIVER'S FLAT

CHAPTER 37
LOCATING THE BANK

The next day, Henry was in Memphis before Leduc opened his pawn shop. He killed time by dropping into Sammy's clothing store on Front Street. He purchased two silk shirts with his usual discount and visited with Sammy a while.

Leduc was surprised when Henry appeared as he was unlocking the front door. "What's up?" he asked.

Henry said, "We need to talk."

Henry gazed into the display counters as Leduc's helpers arrived and opened the store for the day. Then he followed Leduc to his office in the back. He showed Leduc the numbers from Marvin's hat and asked, "Are these numbers on that list from the watch box that you showed me at the September Club?"

Leduc rummaged through a desk drawer and pulled the list out. He exclaimed, "Yes, they are!"

The Musician remarked, "I'll say these numbers mean more than the others. Marvin's hat was more important to him than his wallet or mandolin. That would be his safe spot for a valued note!"

DRIVER'S FLAT

Leduc called his local banker and asked him for the location of the bank that was assigned the number on Marvin's note.

He hung up, looked at Henry and said, "It's a bank in Driver's Flat, Mississippi."

The two put their heads together and concluded that there had to be an important reason why Marvin had kept this one bank number separate from the two other unidentified banks on the list.

Leduc asked Henry if he had made any headway on identifying the people in the photograph.

Henry said, "No. But that's my next project. Let me snoop around and case that bank and see if anyone there ever dealt with Marvin. I need to hurry because this bank and two more are on the list that Popov has."

As Henry was driving east on Poplar in light traffic, it came to him that the lady in the picture had grown up in Driver's Flat! He decided to visit the little town.

First, he pulled into a mall parking lot to make a call. He made contact with a friend from his old days in Memphis. For years, they had been regulars at the Crimson Feather supper club. They chatted a while. Then Henry asked, "Do you remember Agnes Biffle?"

His friend said, "Hey, you know better than that! She was the longtime hostess at the Crimson Feather. But it was her daughter, Shirley Biffle, who I remember best. In her prime, Shirley was the most beautiful stripper in town: long legs, good tan, big boobs. And she wasn't pneumatic! I never knew why she chose the stage name of *Nevaeh*."

DRIVER'S FLAT

Henry chuckled. "I do. She told me late one night at a wild party that it's *Heaven* spelled backwards. She said that's where she wanted the club patrons to think they were after they watched her dance!"

His friend agreed, "I was in love with her, but I could never get her to go out with me. She was in her prime when she quit dancing at the Clothes-Hangers Gentleman's Club to work as a flight attendant at Delta. She liked flying better; there her attention came from wealthier and more refined men."

"Do you know where Agnes is now?" asked Henry.

"Yes. After she retired, she went to stay at her sister's house across the line at Driver's Flat. I have the address."

Henry headed out of Memphis down I-22 to the Driver's Flat exit. After a few turns, he arrived at a small white house a few blocks from the picturesque downtown. He was expected, since his friend had called ahead. Agnes' sister, Jan Moore, was already at the glass door looking for him. She was a tiny, elderly, gray-haired lady. Henry was invited into her living room where hot tea and scones were on the coffee table.

Jan spoke, "My sister passed away last year. I remember you from the Crimson Feather. I was there a lot with my sister. I thought you were so good-looking!"

Henry reddened.

He handed her a copy of the club picture. "Do you recognize the man?" he inquired.

She placed the back of her hand over her mouth and squealed, "Why, that's Marvin Fant! I haven't seen him in years. And, of course, Agnes."

Henry took the picture back and stared. He hadn't known Marvin at the time the picture was made, but he could see the resemblance now.

DRIVER'S FLAT

Jan added, "After Agnes moved back here, Marvin would stop by if he was hitchhiking in the area. He always had a present or flowers for her. I think he was sweet on Agnes. He met her at the Crimson Feather years ago."

"Do you recognize the toy in the picture?"

"Yes, indeed. When my niece Shirley started flying, she and her little girl, Carol Jean, stayed here with me. Marvin visited here one Christmas with the whole family. He pulled the toy from his leather bag and let the girl play with it. The child had so much fun with the toy, Marvin let it stay here for years until Carol Jean left for college."

"What happened to it?"

Henry noticed the sister's body become tense.

"I'm not sure. He said he was going to put it in a lockbox in our bank. You know, the bank was robbed last year. They said a lot of the lockboxes were broken into. The law found out from the owners that really nothing was taken."

Jan stopped and poured more tea for them. "There was one big box that was empty, but they couldn't find out who the owner was. It was rented a long time ago when you didn't have to give a name. The bank issued the key and whoever came to the bank and showed the key for the box would be allowed to enter. I hope Marvin's toy wasn't in that box."

The Musician's heart sank.

"What was the toy like?"

"Oh! It had to be expensive. It was gold. About the size of a large goose egg. It was beautiful! It had diamond and ruby clusters all round it. Real diamonds and rubies."

"Wow!" exclaimed Henry.

"There was a small door on the side. Inside was a surprise - a little golden hen picking up a sapphire egg from its nest. The little egg was a pendant that could be worn."

"Did Marvin ever say where he got this?"

"No. Agnes had asked him about it. He just smiled and said it was very valuable and that it would be his retirement one day."

Jan continued, "Agnes made a lot of friends at the club. A while back, another man dropped by to visit. He didn't know she had passed."

"Oh?" Henry's interest peaked.

"Yes. He said he was a regular at the club before she retired. I didn't know him. We just stood out on the porch and talked."

"Maybe I knew him. What was his name?"

"You know, I never asked."

"Was he short and balding?" asked Henry.

"No. He was a tall, lanky man with a beard."

Henry groaned. Popov! Somehow he had managed to identify Agnes and locate her address.

"Did he talk about the old days?" asked Henry.

"Yes. We found out both of us had been in the club one night when Carl Perkins played, before he became famous, or so the man said. He asked if any other regulars had stayed in touch with Agnes. I told him Agnes would get cards and calls from her friends and that her most frequent visitor was Marvin."

Thoughtfully, Henry asked, "Was that man's visit before or after the bank robbery?"

"Oh. It was a few weeks before."

With the scone dish empty, Henry said goodbye. Jan followed him out on the porch, where Henry noticed that the front of the local bank was visible.

Henry was convinced that he and Leduc were on to something big. Then he felt a chill! Popov knew, or suspected, what the toy was and would be trying to pinpoint its location.

Henry had a good suspicion of what it was. He adored gold, diamonds, and fine jewelry. He also kept abreast of famous thefts of valuables that had occurred over the years. Marvin's toy could be a certain object that had disappeared over a hundred years ago.

Henry was full of questions... no answers.

CHAPTER 38
INSIDE THE VAULT

Before Henry traveled far, his phone rang. A female spoke in a hushed voice, "Henry, you don't know me. But I'm with Esker. He's hurt very bad and wants to see you. We're in Memphis."

Henry asked for directions.

She said, "Be low-key, and check out the neighborhood on your way."

Esker, a/k/a "Big" Esker, was from Massachusetts. He had served a hitch in the Federal Correctional Institute in west Tennessee with Henry ten years ago. Esker had a long history of holding up armored cars and banks. Henry wondered what he was doing in Memphis.

The Musician knew the Midtown locale well. The area was used quite often by a variety of crooks to dodge the law. He parked his pink Cadillac in front of an office building in East Memphis and called a taxi to carry him to a rental car company where he chose a plain Ford.

Soon, he arrived at an older house that stretched from one side of the narrow lot to the other, offering an entrance from either street. Henry pulled his ball cap brim low and quickly stepped up on the back porch. He knocked on the door, and a big blonde girl with a generous chest and radiant blue eyes ushered him in. She introduced herself as Bea. Admiring her shapely backside, he followed her down a hall to a den. Seated in a brown recliner, Esker had a bloody bandage around his left shoulder.

Esker was a large, dark-haired man with a strong torso. Henry hadn't seen him in a while and was shocked at his obvious weight loss. Esker grinned at him, but his handshake was weak.

They briefly talked about their prison hitch. Esker coughed violently and strangled. "I need help. And I'm asking you because I know you don't rat out."

The Musician nodded.

Esker continued, "I got invited on a bank heist just before Christmas. It was a small town near here. Driver's Flat. My job was to drill the vault door and lockboxes. I have the latest equipment. I knew one of the guys from my Boston days. Barely. The job went down as planned except some lawman showed up just as we were finishing. He took a wild shot, and I was hit."

"I know they didn't take you to the emergency room?"

"Nope," Esker grimaced as he changed position. "That never happens."

"Where did they take you?"

Esker laughed, "They made some calls and were directed to a vet that was going through an expensive divorce!"

"I guess when you get well, you'll be chasing cars down the street."

"That's funny!" Esker said, through a series of painful coughs. "Henry, I need you to help protect me on my share of the heist, and I'll cut you in."

"Okay," said Henry. With Esker, there was no need to discuss the split.

"The boss man and Wiley, the guy I knew, went to the bank's back door and made the rest of us wait for a signal.

Wiley easily got the door open and let me and the other two in. One stayed just inside the door as a lookout. I did my work. I had no trouble torching the vault door or drilling the lockboxes. I had my back turned most of the time as I worked. There were large stacks of new currency in the room. The others quickly took it out. There was some old money in a corner that they didn't bother. The boss man was looking at the contents of each big lockbox as they were opened. He cussed when I opened one box. It was empty. After that, he seemed disinterested in my drilling and told me not to fool with the small boxes."

"Running out of time?"

"Yeah. But then I heard a clamor at the back of the vault. I heard one of the team say, 'What in the hell is this?' They had forced the lock on a closet door. I looked over my shoulder and saw stacks of Lucky Charms boxes on a pallet. The other guy ripped one open and it was full of old bills. All four of us stared!"

"Cereal boxes?" asked Henry.

"Yeah. The boss man exclaimed, "What the hell is this? What have we come across?' They discussed whether or not to take the pallet. One guy said, 'Why not? We need more to show for our efforts. We have room in our vehicle.' They quickly loaded the pallet in the getaway van."

"Who took you to the vet?"

"The boss man. I don't think that gang is local because he had to make several calls to arrange the vet visit. After I was patched up, he picked up Bea and brought us here. She is to take care of me. She's a private nurse. A few days later, he brought me my cut of the new currency. I was instructed to stay low until I get well."

"If you got your cut, why do you need me?"

Esker coughed violently. "I don't know if I'm going to make it. I got a kid in Boston to take care of. I've been on these heists before. But this one was strange. I've never done a bank this small. How much money could be in a small town? From the body language I saw inside the vault and the different remarks made by the gang, I think they were more interested in drilling lockboxes than stealing cash. I've thought about the robbery since, and I'm convinced that they came for something that wasn't there. But my deal was to get a cut of all they were after. These guys were too professional. I think they were hired to do the heist."

"Would you recognize them again?"

"If the law asked that, the answer would be, 'No.'"

"Again, why do you need me?"

"You know more about what's going on behind the scenes than anyone I've ever met. Since they didn't want those small boxes opened and had me quit drilling after the empty box, I think that box was their target. See if you can find out what was supposed to be in that box and where it might be."

"That might take some time."

"If I don't make it, promise me you'll get my share to my kid."

"You got it."

"And be careful. One guy inside with us didn't seem to have been in a bank vault before. He came across as a button man for a dry-cleaner up the line."

"Really?"

"Yeah. I've wondered if that box had not been empty, me or Wiley, or the boss man, or all of us would have been whacked."

"Maybe he was to take the loot and deliver it elsewhere."

"Could be."

Henry asked, "Do you remember the number of that last box?"

"Usually, I'm concentrating on my drilling and the numbers aren't important anyway. But this one I did because it was the number of my jersey I wore playing American Legion baseball: 15."

Bea took Henry to the door. Out of the blue she asked, "Do you not like women?"

Caught by surprise, Henry blurted, "Yes! Why?"

"When I led you down the hall, I didn't feel much heat from your eyeballs. My good-looking body deserves extra!"

Red-faced, Henry replied, "Touché," and added, "You should talk to Phyllis, my third ex-wife."

"Why her?"

"I married her twice. She knows more."

"Do you ever hear from her?"

"Yeah. She writes me letters all the time wanting me back."

"I'd love to read them."

Henry laughed and replied, "I don't think so. The love words would make you blush!"

"Not with my track record."

Bea smiled and winked as she shut the door.

As Henry walked to his car, he thought that Bea, the rented nurse, had gained the upper hand with him. Esker had probably put her up to mess with him. He was satisfied that Esker was in good hands.

CHAPTER 39
THE PROBE

As Henry drove through Oxford on the way home, he stopped at Wal-Mart and bought a burner phone. He dialed Esker's number. After Bea put him on the phone, Henry asked, "Did you get your cut of the cereal box money?"

Esker replied, "No. I asked for it, and the boss man said I might get it later. He had been told by his contact that the money wasn't going to be split until the owners were identified. The folks up the line are uneasy with having this money."

Henry immediately thought that the robbers were afraid that taking the cereal boxes would infuriate whoever had stashed them in the bank. Maybe a rival mob.

When Henry entered his driveway, the moon was shining brightly. He stopped short of his carport, pulled out his laptop, and checked his security system for alerts of any intruder. None.

After he ate a light meal, he called his contact in Las Vegas and reported his conversation with Agnes' sister. The voice on the other end whistled with excitement. After a few minutes of

DRIVER'S FLAT

his explanation of what the toy could be, the needle on Henry's excitement meter hit the forward peg.

"Wow!" exclaimed Henry.

"Yeah. There is a standing offer for the artifact if it can be produced undamaged. Doesn't matter if the ownership is hot, or otherwise!"

"How much?"

The voice hesitated, "A similar object, that was found at a flea market in Kansas five years ago, transferred for at least thirty-three million. The buyer at the flea market only paid $14,000 for it and a couple of appraisals didn't add much to the purchase price."

"Man, I need to get busy! That would pay off my wife's credit cards!"

The voice laughed. "Boy, you ain't right!" He knew Henry was on his eighth wife and had a reputation of allowing each one to spend more as the marriages progressed.

Henry made a call to a local lawyer who had probated Marvin's estate. He was told that the sole devisee was a nephew who owned an older motel in Vicksburg. When asked, the lawyer provided the nephew's number and added, "I located a substantial amount of monies in a number of banks. The nephew knew very little of Marvin's business. Neither of us think that we located all of them. There's no telling how much of Marvin's money will never be found."

"How did you find those accounts?" asked Henry.

"Marvin had his statements sent to his sister who lives in Chickasaw County who forwarded them to me. But some banks around the country don't mail out statements until there is activity in the account."

Henry thanked the lawyer for the information, told his current wife he would be back later, and headed to Vicksburg.

DRIVER'S FLAT

Henry was seated at a corner table in the restaurant of the Redwood Inn, his back to the oak-paneled wall, enjoying a slice of lemon meringue pie and coffee. Across the table the owner, Rocky Rossi, who had grown up in the part of Chickasaw County near Cade County, was catching up with news from home and about friends he had in common with Henry.

Rocky guessed that all of Marvin's money probably hadn't been found. Henry asked if he knew of Marvin having any jewelry.

"Just a bunch of old watches that he bought in pawnshops around the country," laughed Rocky.

Henry told him about Marvin having a lockbox at the bank in Driver's Flat that was opened in the robbery. Then he cautiously asked, "If he had anything in that box that was valuable and I could find it, would you share?"

Rocky laughed loudly. "Oh, sure. Uncle Marvin never cared about things. Just money. I doubt he had any jewelry in that box."

"How would you share?" asked the Musician, going back to his question.

Rocky rubbed his chin and took a gulp of coffee as he answered, "Hey, look. I've done good over the years with this motel. I'm well off. Your search of finding anything is a long shot. Give me a fourth and you can keep the rest."

They shook hands. Henry left.

The next day Henry moved around the area looking for Marvin's friends. He went to nearby Houston, Mississippi, and talked to the funeral director who had transported Marvin's body back home for the funeral. He provided several names.

Then he remarked, "I picked up Marvin's personal belongings. When I asked the funeral home owner where Marvin's mandolin was, I got a blank stare. I smelled a rat. The owner got real nervous when I explained that Marvin was never without his instrument, and it wasn't on the inventory.

"The owner called in a shifty assistant and chastised him. The guy muttered that he would look around. In a few minutes he came back with it in his hand. I also asked about Marvin's hat, which was his trademark. I was convinced that they didn't have it. Must have been left on the side of the interstate."

Henry didn't disclose that he knew where it was. He asked, "How did you find out Marvin had been killed on the highway?"

"Oh, his friend Irv Lackey at Four Points called me with the news. He said a funeral home in Memphis had phoned him. But I never thought to ask Irv how they knew to get up with him."

DRIVER'S FLAT

CHAPTER 40
THE MUSICIAN'S MOVE

Henry's TV was turned on to the news, but he wasn't watching. He was in deep thought about Marvin's toy. At the moment, he knew more about it than Leduc or Popov. They had only seen an old picture, but he now had a description of its details.

According to his Las Vegas pawnshop contact, the toy, if it was what he suspected, had never been photographed while in the hands of its original owner. Art collectors all over the world wanted the object and would pay dearly for it. Of course, the toy would have to be located and then authenticated.

Henry the Musician was worried if he had been too generous with potential partners. He had the rights of ownership by virtue of his deal with Marvin's heir, who would get a fourth. Henry had committed five percent to Tony. He would have to work out an arrangement with Leduc, who had put him on the trail.

And, then there was Esker, his old cellmate. Esker would not have a claim if Henry found it before the bank robbery gang did. The value of Esker's tip was that the toy was still unfound, which was the basis of his search. He decided he would do Esker right if he located the item.

While in prison, Esker disclosed that he had mostly robbed armored cars in the Boston and Charlestown areas. His favorite heist story was about the Isabella Stewart Gardner Museum theft in Boston. Works of art valued at 500 million dollars were stolen and never recovered. Moreover, the robbers had never been caught. The FBI investigation went on for years. The Boston mafia was their primary focus. Esker laughed when he told the Musician that he knew who had removed the paintings from the museum, but he didn't know for sure who had ordered the heist or who the mastermind was. He said he had been a suspect but denied being involved. One night, he told the Musician he knew where the paintings had been sent. He said the order for specific paintings on exhibit in the museum had been received from overseas.

Henry reasoned that since the bank robbers, including Esker, were most likely from the Boston area, it made sense that the same bunch of folks involved in the art heist could be behind the search for Marvin's toy. He would have to be careful with Esker about his search. He didn't need the Boston crowd to be aware that he was their competitor. That gang could direct serious heat toward him.

Henry knew about Irv Lackey, the hitchhiker's friend. Henry had lucked into a substantial finder's fee the year before for locating a small fortune belonging to a local man. The man had died, leaving only clues as to where the bulk of his wealth might be. Others had been involved with him in the search, including Deputy Sheriff Wade Hampton. Irv had provided the key clue to Deputy Hampton of its location.

Henry found Irv's number in the directory and dialed. The phone rang a while but no one answered. Later, Henry dialed again. No answer. The next day, he dialed Irv's number several times. Still, no answer. Henry dialed all week. No answer. He tried different hours of the day and night. No luck. He began to wonder if Irv was dead, in the hospital, visiting relatives, or if the telephone line was down. Irv was too old to be working offshore on an oil rig or on a distant construction job.

Henry didn't know where Irv lived, so he called his former fortune-hunting partner Deputy Hampton. Wade laughed when Henry told about not getting an answer and of his concern about Irv's welfare. He chortled. "That old coot is alive and well. I saw him in Central City a couple of days ago buying groceries. He has caller ID and refuses to answer any call from a strange number or if he just doesn't want to be bothered. Why do you need to get up with him, of all people?"

Henry explained to Wade that he was on the trail of a missing object that could be very valuable. Henry trusted Wade, so he disclosed the information that he had about Marvin's death and the later bank robbery of the Driver's Flat bank and speculated that Irv could be a confidant of Marvin.

Wade replied, "I knew Marvin all my life. Like everybody else around here, I've often picked him up on the side of the road. It makes sense that Irv would be a friend of Marvin's. Irv and Marvin shared the same degree of peculiarity."

"Where does he live? I'd like to visit him. I want to know how the funeral home director in Memphis knew to call him."

"He lives a mile northeast of Four Points. I've got to serve some papers on a court witness out there. I'll pick you up when I come through town."

As they rode to Four Points, a village just south of Central City near the Webster County line, Wade described Irv as a loner who had raised his five kids after his wife died. He told Henry that Irv spent time in the military, and he told about the man's unparalleled honesty, his disdain of politicians, his frugality, and that he didn't own a vehicle.

DRIVER'S FLAT

"How does he get around?" asked Henry.

"He catches rides with neighbors. He usually walks to the store in Four Points, and hangs around until someone heads to Central City. That's about the extent of his travels."

Wade served his summons in Four Points and headed to Irv's. He turned onto a gravel road and traveled a mile to Irv's dirt driveway. His ramshackle, lap-sided wooden house sat upon a rise a short distance from the road. The planks were weathered, and the rusty, tin-covered roof dated to the Depression. Across one side of the front porch, a stack of wood was waiting to be burned in his cookstove. Wade cautioned Henry, "When we get there, let me knock on the door. You'll make him suspicious. You might not like how he smells. He doesn't bathe that often."

Wade parked, and they left the vehicle. Wade walked up the wooden steps of the porch. Henry stopped a few yards from the porch's edge. A nice breeze was coming around the corner of the house, sending music from a couple of wind chimes on one end of the porch. Wade rapped his knuckles against a porch post. He could see Irv approach the screen door from inside the front room. He was a short, scrawny, unshaven man with a protuberant Adam's apple. Irv stopped a couple of feet short of the screen door and spoke, "Howdy, Wade."

Wade stared at a carton of soft drinks and a paper grocery bag leaning against the porch wall by the door.

"Been to town, Irv?"

"Yeah. Just now got here. Caught a ride with my neighbor, Carl Vance, and he let me off down at the mailbox. Whatcha doing out this way?"

"Just making a welfare check on several folks. Glad to see you, Irv."

"Take it easy, Wade."

As Wade turned to step down off the porch, he noticed Henry staring at the larger wind chime. Both men slowly walked back to the truck and got in. Wade backed his truck around and headed to the road. He urgently said, "Irv's in trouble!"

"How do you know?"

"Carl Vance has been dead for years. And I could see melted ice cream coming out of the grocery sack bottom. Irv has a weakness for ice cream, and he wouldn't forget to put it in his fridge."

"Someone is in the house. When a gust of wind turned that big, shiny disc on the bottom of the wind chime, I could see the reflection of the rear end of a black pickup parked behind Irv's barn," observed Henry.

Wade concluded, "That makes sense. Irv stood back from the door. That means someone was flattened against the wall so they could watch his face to keep him from sending a signal with his lips or eyes."

Two sets of eyes watched the truck leave. When satisfied they were alone, a powerfully-built man quizzed Irv, "Okay, old man, where is it?"

"What?"

The man replied, "I don't know what, but you do. It's what your hitchhiker friend left for you to keep."

"Well, you ain't gittin' it."

The second man hit Irv in his mouth. Blood squirted. The blow knocked him onto his sofa.

Irv replied bleakly, "Okay. Don't hit me again. It's over in that cabinet against the wall."

Both intruders eyeballed the glass-enclosed curio cabinet. Each shelf was filled with objects. The slim man strode to the case followed by his pal and jerked one door open. They froze as they both saw for an instant a thin silver wire going from the door latch through the top of the cabinet, upwards into the ceiling.

The big intruder screamed, "No!" but his voice was muffled as a trap door dropped down, releasing barrels of dirty gravel on top of the two men. The weight of the rocks slammed both to the floor, partially covering them. When they struggled from underneath, coughing from the clouds of dust and clearing their eyes, they stared at Irv, who had a shotgun aimed at them.

As they broke for the back door, Irv pumped three shells through the gun's action.

Wade parked his vehicle around the curve. He told Henry he would cut through the woods and jog to the house. Wade took his shotgun out of the rack, gave it to Henry, and told him to guard the road.

Wade slipped through trees. As he was nearing the house, he heard the blast of a shotgun and a scream. The sounds were followed by two more shots. He glimpsed two men in black clothes flee out the back door and run toward the barn. Before Wade got out of the woods, the pickup sped out of the driveway turning away from Henry at the driveway's end.

Henry was slumped in the seat peering over the edge of the dash. Henry saw the black vehicle before he heard it. As the pickup turned onto the road, the driver pulled his mask off. He never saw Henry in Wade's vehicle. He was an albino, with his long blond hair tied in a knot behind his head. Henry gawked. He recognized the driver, Jason Bates! He knew him to be a button man for Attila, the enforcer for the old State Line Mob, and he had an idea who his partner was: Dago. They were inseparable. Jason was a card-carrying psycho who loved to torture, just for fun; Dago was just downright mean. Both hung

DRIVER'S FLAT

out at the September Club and socialized with Henry. He knew they worked as a team.

A few years back, a headless skeleton had been discovered in a steel drum in the Mississippi River near Memphis. The body was believed by the public to be a cousin of Jason's who had suddenly disappeared. According to strong rumors, Jason had killed the cousin's mother-in-law, and the cousin had refused to pay him the agreed fee. The rumors also gave Jason and Dago credit for the hit. Why were they interested in this old miser? They were supposed to be locating the mastermind of the truck heist.

Wade hollered, "Irv, are you okay?"

Irv replied weakly, "Better than them two thugs."

Wade entered the house closely followed by Henry, who had driven back to the house. Irv was seated on the floor, his battered face covered in blood. A 12 gauge shotgun was in his lap; empty hulls lay nearby. The room was filled with dust and a huge pile of rocks in the corner.

Henry retrieved a first aid kit from the pickup, and Wade treated the cuts. "What is this all about, Irv? I didn't know you had enemies," he seriously questioned the injured Irv.

"I didn't. Until today, that is."

"Tell us what happened."

"When I got home, those two men were already in my house. They had gone through all my drawers and closets. They grabbed me and asked, 'Where is it?'" Irv rubbed blood from his lips onto his already dirty overalls.

"I asked 'What?' They said, 'We don't know what, but you do.' About that time y'all drove up. One man stood against the wall with a pistol. He warned me not to give you any signals and said for me to get rid of y'all."

Holding his throbbing head in his hands, Irv continued, "After y'all left, they started hitting me and kept on asking if I knowed where my hitchhiker friend put whatever he took out of his lockbox at the bank in Driver's Flat. They knocked me down by my couch. I told them what they were looking for was in my cabinet over in the corner. When they opened its door, my booby trap was triggered. The rocks knocked them to the floor."

With a grin of satisfaction, Irv moved his arms into a shooting position. He explained, "I pulled my shotgun from under the couch where I hide it and started shooting. I burned them butts good with rocksalt as they ran out of the house! They'll be standing up for a long time while they eat."

"Was Marvin Fant your friend?"

"Yep. Longtime."

Wade said, "This man with me is Henry Childs. He is also looking for what those robbers were. The object belongs to Marvin's nephew, and he gave Henry rights to find Marvin's possessions."

"I knowed Rocky when he was growing up. Fine young fellow. I been waiting to hear from him ever since Marvin was buried."

"Why?"

"'Cause I got something that belongs to Marvin. Don't know why he hasn't called me or come by."

"Would Rocky know you have it?"

"Well, nah. Not unless Marvin told him." Irv admitted.

"How are you and Marvin friends?"

"We're distant cousins. Back in the old days, our families lived in the same community sorta south of Vena. We went to the same school where Marvin's mother was a teacher. Of course, I was a good bit older than Marvin. About ten years. When I got grown, I joined the army and got sent to the war. I lost track of Marvin for a while."

"Vietnam?" asked Wade.

"Nah. You're off one war. The back end of that Korean mess."

Wade smiled. "I was there. In the front part. A Marine. Cold, wasn't it?"

"You got that right. I still shiver in July." Irv continued, "Marvin used to stay here when he came through catching rides. When my kids were still home, he used to bring them presents from up north - things you can't get around here. Plus, pecan candy from the coast. He had lots to tell. I knew more about what was going on from him than watching that idiot box over there."

"Can we get Marvin's property?" asked Henry. "Rocky agreed that he would get a part if I could get anything of Marvin's sold."

"You shore can. I don't want what's not mine or something I could get kilt over. You'll have to go get it 'cause I don't feel good right now. Go down to my chicken house. It's down in the middle of a barrel of peanuts that I saved years and years ago to plant. I never did."

"Why did you use the peanut barrel for a hiding place?" asked Wade.

"Who would bother to mess with a barrel of ruined peanuts?" emphasized Irv.

Wade and Henry walked to the chicken house and opened a wire gate. Wade cautioned, "Watch where you step."

Henry grinned. He didn't want to soil his crocodile loafers.

At one end of the shack against a rickety wall were barrels of feed with wooden planks over their tops. A flock of nosy, "banty" hens, led by an aggressive rooster, ran toward them, thinking they were going to be fed early. They shooed the hens away and found the peanut barrel. Wade cautiously ran his arm up to his elbow into the dusty hulls and felt a large object. He pulled out a ragged burlap towsack. Then he reached inside and slowly pulled out a small, wooden box with a hinged lid on its top.

"What's this?" asked Henry.

"I dunno. Let's open it in front of Irv so he can be a witness," replied Wade.

They walked back to Irv's house. He had cleaned his face and was seated at the kitchen table drinking a tall glass of iced tea. Wade placed the box on the table and asked Irv, "Do you know what's in here?"

"I shore do."

Wade opened the box and gasped! He heard Henry suck wind!

On its side lay a jeweled and ridged yellow gold egg. It was about five inches high and three inches wide. Wade carefully lifted the object free from the box and placed it on an accompanying pedestal. Henry and Wade were speechless. Henry, a lover of fine jewelry, had never seen a piece as exquisite. His eyes bugged!

There was a door on the egg's side. Henry carefully opened it and stared. The inside was just as Agnes' sister had described: a little golden hen picking up a sapphire egg from its nest. He could see that the little egg was a pendant that could be worn. The large egg was covered with clusters of diamonds and rubies. It was obvious the egg had great value!

Wade asked, "Irv, do you know where Marvin got this egg?"

"He traded a Rolex watch for it."

"Oh?"

"Marvin had a building in New York City where he rented out rooms. This lady ran it for part of the profits. He would stay there when he was in that area."

Irv enjoyed knowing and telling them the story of Marvin's trade.

"According to Marvin, an old man had boarded there for years, and they became friends. The old man was a retired merchant marine whose ship, a passenger liner, had plied the waters of the Black Sea in 1939. His ship was laid up in Odessa for repairs. One night as he left the bar that he frequented, he was approached by a well-dressed Russian Jew named Shawl Dessler. The Russian had recognized, by his uniform, that the man was the ship's purser and head steward. The Jew was desperate to flee the country with his wife and young daughter. The town was full of refugees fleeing the turmoil in Europe and threats of war and were looking for safe passage. Slots on ships were filled."

Irv sat back in his chair and took another swig of tea. "Marvin said the Russian begged to get his family on the ship. He had very little money, but he offered the egg if the purser would board his family. The purser was overwhelmed by the desperation in the eyes of the mother and the scared look on the face of the little girl. His ship was already overcrowded, but there was a small cabin on a below deck filled with supplies which could be stored elsewhere."

Irv took out a large bandana and wiped his face.

"He gave in and the wife hugged him as they went aboard to sail. The travel documents of the family only allowed them to travel to Portugal, but with the aid of an assistant, the purser was able to trick the papers so the family was able to enter the United States through the harbor in New York City."

Wade interrupted, "Did the purser know where the Jew got the egg?"

"Yes. The purser was able to visit with the family during the voyage. Shawl Dessler said his father was a guard at the Grand Palace when it was ransacked by the Bolsheviks in 1917. The palace was looted by a drunken, unruly mob. He snatched the egg from a thief and fled, with the intent to return it to the Tsar when peace was restored. That never happened because the royal family was executed. Other eggs and valuables were stored by the Bolsheviks at the Kremlin in Moscow. In the 1920s and 1930s, the Russian economy tanked. The government started selling the Imperial eggs to international dealers for quick rubles. The father kept the egg because he feared execution for having it. Before he died, he gave it to his son, Shawl."

Irv had to catch his breath to finish his tale. He rested back in his seat.

"The purser had no family except for a grandson who was about to graduate from college. He tried to sell the egg, but he never got an offer for more than what the gold was worth at the time. So he traded the egg to Marvin for the diamond-studded Rolex to give his grandson as a graduation gift. For a while, Marvin kept the egg in his leather bag as he traveled. He liked to show it off to pretty women he met in his travels."

Irv continued his narrative, "Marvin made a mistake one time in Miami. He went into a jewelry store in a seedy part of town to shop for used watches. When he pulled the egg from his bag to show it off, he noticed that the jeweler got uptight. When the jeweler tried to buy the egg and kept bumping his offers, Marvin realized he was holding a valuable piece. He noticed a tough in the background of the store listening to the conversation."

With a sly grin on his face, Irv told more about Marvin.

"Marvin was in Miami to get a check-up by a doctor he had used before. He had rented a room nearby. At the doctor's office, he was asked for a stool specimen, which he was unable to produce. The nurse assured him that he was not the only one who couldn't. She handed him a box, told him to get a sample at home, and drop the box off at the office."

Continuing the story, Irv explained, "When he left the doctor's office, Marvin dropped into a second-hand store and bought a large purse. As he made his way to his room, he was certain he was being followed by the tough from the jewelry store. The next day, after considerable trouble trying all night, he was able to get a specimen for the box. He put the container into the old purse and headed to the bus stop for a ride to the doctor's office. He wasn't about to be seen carrying the white box on the street because everyone he encountered would recognize his mission."

Smiling broadly and showing that a few teeth were missing, Irv crossed his legs. He said, "As he waited for the bus on the busy sidewalk, the same tough that had followed him the day before, grabbed the purse from his hand and swiftly fled. Marvin chased him, bellowing, 'No! No! Come back. That's too valuable! Bring it back!' The robber got away, grinning over his shoulder as he ran, 'Sorry buddy, but this snatch is my ticket to Fat City!'"

Wade interrupted, "So the thief got the crap?"

"It then occurred to Marvin that someone wanted his egg very badly. He went back to his room, gathered his belongings, and caught a Greyhound to Memphis. He laughed all the way, thinking about the looks that would come over the faces of the thief and the jeweler when they opened the box, expecting to see a shiny, gold egg covered in jewels!" exclaimed Irv.

Henry laughed so long that Irv thought that his tickle-box had turned over.

"He left it for years with a trusted friend near Memphis while he traveled. Then he put it in a lockbox at some bank."

"How did you come by it?" asked Wade.

"Marvin said he got to thinking that he might die and nobody would know its location. He trusted me, so he took it from the bank and asked me to keep it. He said when he decided to quit traveling, he would sell it."

"How long have you been keeping it?"

"'Bout thirty years."

Wade complimented Irv, "You did good getting the upper hand on those thugs."

"Yeah. Just like I did those Commies in Korea one night in the snow when a squad of sappers tried to sneak into our lines to cut the throats of any sleeping soldier they could find."

As Henry and Wade walked out, Irv called, "I need help re-setting my trap. I've got to have that to stay ahead of any vagabonds that don't mean well. I'm too old to crawl around in that hot attic. It took me most of a day to arm it before."

"You got it, Irv. We owe you a lot," said Wade.

Henry winked at Wade and asked, "Say, Irv, do you have any other traps?"

Irv smiled at him through bruised lips.

After they were satisfied Irv didn't need medical attention, Wade and Henry the Musician left the house with the box.

On the way to the truck, Wade remarked, "When the pickup left Irv's, I could hardly hear it."

"I noticed that, too."

"That has to be the same two men who were at the lake camp and who confronted L.C. I wonder why it was so quiet. Do you know?"

Henry replied, "Yeah. They have tires with special treads. They run a certain type of synthetic oil in the motor after they add some Sea Foam, and they remove the windshield wipers to reduce wind noise."

"Oh, I've never heard about that," said Wade. "I'll bet that same truck shoved the Driver's Flat banker into Enid Lake."

Henry perked up. He knew about the banker's car going into the lake but not that it had been shoved. So, Atilla's men were not just after the hijacked cargo but the egg as well.

CHAPTER 41
THE EGG'S IDENTITY

"What are you going to do now?" asked Wade as they rode to Poston.

"I'm going to take some pictures and visit my pawnbroker friend in Memphis. He should know who to contact to identify the artifact. Can I leave it with you?"

"Sure. That's probably the safest place you could find. There is always someone in the sheriff's office around the clock."

The next day, Henry walked into Leduc's pawn shop with photographs of the artwork.

Leduc whistled, "Where did you find this?"

"Where it's been for the last thirty years," smirked the Musician. "In a feed barrel at the back end of a chicken house that belongs to a friend of the old man who was in your picture."

Leduc felt a sinking feeling hit his stomach. Henry possessed the egg and had the upper hand. Henry could control any divvy.

DRIVER'S FLAT

Henry said, "Don't worry. We're in this together. I found it, but you're needed to help locate an appraiser and a buyer."

"Let's go down the street and talk to Albert Peacock. Maybe he can identify the egg."

Henry squirmed. "I didn't think of him."

Albert was an elderly goldsmith whose shop was in the back of the Sugar Rush jewelry store located on the edge of the Beale Street complex of bars and nightclubs. Henry knew him well, for he was the one who had designed his butterfly ring. The Sugar Rush sold downscale wedding rings, cheap gold chains, and inexpensive watches, which was very profitable. Henry knew the store was a front for Albert's main activity of melting gold and silver jewelry to create exquisite art objects. Years ago, Albert had served a prison sentence for receiving stolen goods from local fences. At the time, he was down on his luck from having to provide for his ailing parents, who were World War II immigrants. Although an Englishman, Albert's father had been a superb goldsmith in Germany for the Huettemann family in the Dusseldorf area. While ill, he had taught Albert his trade before he died.

Since his prison release, Albert had taken a more clever approach to his inventory acquisition. He didn't want to go back. Through prison contacts, he was able to order the amount of gold he needed through a front man. He didn't want to know the source.

Albert then created decorative objects as requested by leading designers and jewelry houses. These pieces sold for large sums, and some were displayed in top-tier museums. Unfortunately, because of his prison record, none of the buyers could give him credit as being the artist. As he didn't pawn or buy any of his retail inventory from customers, his records were never checked.

DRIVER'S FLAT

Leduc and Henry were buzzed through a back door into Albert's foundry. Albert had just finished a job and was sitting at his bench drinking a 7 Up and eating a lemon tart.

"Would you look at these pictures and see if this object might have value?" asked Leduc.

Albert took one look and exclaimed, "Holy Moses! Where did you get these?" Without waiting for an answer, he grabbed a powerful jeweler's glass and intently studied the first photograph. They watched him with interest. A pro at work. He studied every detail of the egg. Then he examined the pictures of the objects from the egg's interior.

Albert carefully placed the loupe on the table, looked from Leduc to Henry and asked, "Could I surmise that y'all have this piece of artwork in your possession?"

"You surmise correctly," replied Leduc. "It's in a burglar-proof location."

"You lucky guys!" exclaimed Albert.

The Musician blurted, "Do you know its identity?"

"Oh, yes! I most certainly do."

"Tell us."

"It's one of the most sought-after art objects in the entire world! A Faberge' Easter egg! One of these is considered the Mona Lisa of the decorative art world!"

Henry smacked his open hand with a fist. "I suspected that all along."

"Yes. Peter Carl Faberge' was an award-winning master goldsmith who ran the family business, House of Faberge', in Russia's St. Petersburg. In 1885, Tsar Alexander III commissioned him to make a gift for his wife for Easter, with a specific request that it would contain a surprise. So the goldsmith created a white enamel egg which opened to a gold yolk that concealed a small gold hen, which, in turn, opened to a pendant.

"The tsar was so impressed that he had Faberge' make an egg for his wife every Easter after that. Most of them held a surprise inside. Sometimes two would be made in the same year. In all, fifty were made by Faberge'."

After looking at one of the pictures again, Albert continued, "The tsar and his family fled St. Petersburg in 1917 when it was seized by the Bolsheviks. The fifty Imperial eggs were left behind. Ten showed up at the Kremlin Armoury Museum in Moscow. Later eight of those went missing. Others eventually made their way to private dealers. The locations of forty-two are known. Five are believed to have been destroyed, but three are still unaccounted for."

"What about this one?" asked Henry as he pointed to the pictures.

"It has to be the 1886 Imperial Easter egg known as *Hen with Sapphire Pendant*."

"How sure are you?" asked Leduc.

"Mostly sure."

"What makes you believe it's a Faberge' egg to start with?"

Albert held up a trembling hand. "First, let me explain by way of digression. As a young man, my father was a superior jeweler and worked for a goldsmith in London. The company loaned him and two other tradesmen to the Huetteman jewelry business in Dusseldorf, Germany, as apprentices. My father had a knack for sketches. The Huettemans sent him to study under Alma Pihl in Finland in 1939."

"Who was she?" asked Henry.

"She was the granddaughter of Faberge's leading jeweler and the company's first woman designer. She designed the *Winter Egg* in 1913, which is considered the most valuable of all fifty Imperial eggs."

Albert settled back to tell the story. He relayed, "No known photograph or illustration of this egg by its maker or during its display in the Anichkov Palace exists. The 1886 Imperial archive notes this present as 'a hen of gold and rose diamonds taking a sapphire egg out of a nest.'

"The revolution closed the Faberge' workshop, and Alma and her husband fled to Finland. There she taught drawing and calligraphy at a jewelry factory school where my father was a student. In 1940, his last year in her class, Germany invaded France, and, in fear of a European war, my father went back to England. After the war, he came to the States and bought this store from an estate. He specialized in wedding rings. Business was so good, he never bothered to change its name. Later he added a workshop in the back and began to make art objects," stated Albert. Henry and Leduc stared at him almost in disbelief.

He continued, "Alma stayed in contact with him. Just before her death in 1976, she sent my father and her other students the description of all the Imperial eggs that were unaccounted for at that time and asked them to stay on the lookout for any that might show up. I've studied her notes often, and this egg fits the 1886 description."

Henry eagerly asked, "What's it worth?"

Albert hesitated before he recalled, "Groups of these eggs have been exhibited around the world from time to time. Once, an exhibit came to Memphis to the Brooks Museum of Art. I visited the display so often, the security guards became suspicious. They probably thought I was casing the place for a future burglary! Those things are so beautiful! I was envious of the designs and craftsmanship. It took an entire year to make just one.

"I would need to view your egg to assess the quality of the jewels and measure the object's size and weight. A number of the Imperial eggs have been appraised as to the value of the metal alloys and the attached jewels. These appraisals of the alloys and the jewels never amounted to large sums. However, the true value traces back to the art itself. Faberge' rarely used large stones in his pieces. He was quoted that you could spend millions with Tiffany or Cartier to buy large diamonds, but if you wanted to buy a piece of artistic value, you had to buy his because he was the artist jeweler."

Albert's knowledge of the egg's history was evident to the other two men. They made eye contact with each other and both gave a slight nod.

"The last Imperial egg to surface was the *Third Imperial Egg* made in 1887 for the Empress Maria Feodorovna. It was bought at a flea market in the Midwest by a junk dealer. He was about to melt it for scrap, but a quick internet search revealed the egg's identity and that it was worth millions. He sold it for over 30 million, and that egg did have some stones missing."

Henry gasped. Leduc sat down.

Albert continued, "You'll need to have the egg examined by an expert to verify its maker. Every museum and private collector who has the funds will be chomping at the bits to own this one. Will you sell it?"

Henry exclaimed, "Most certainly. Keeping it could get somebody killed!"

"I would recommend putting it on the market through a third-party, so you can remain anonymous," the jeweler advised.

Albert looked around like other people were in the room, lowered his voice, moved closer to Leduc, and spoke, "Popov came by here the day he bought that watch from you and showed me that old picture. The toy looked a lot like an Imperial egg, but there are lots of replications out there. I owe Popov because he is the middleman to the source of my inventory. He said any lost Imperial egg was on his list of various requests from a rich Russian collector. Popov laughed and said that his guy will outbid anyone else for an egg. But if it could be found and stolen by any means, the collector would be happier. That he's gone that route before!"

Henry reflected, "I know why the guy that Esker told me about was in that bank vault. The Russian collector must have placed an order through the Boston mob. With Popov's help, they tracked down Marvin's lady friend's sister. If I'm smart, I'll need to get word back up the line that the egg has been found and is in a safe place. The collector will have to make a legit bid for it."

Henry asked Albert, "Do we owe for your time?"

Albert grinned. "Yes. I want to hold the egg in my hands one time before it goes to a new nest! I promise I won't say 'bak-bak-baaaaak'!"

They laughed and both slapped Albert on his back.

DRIVER'S FLAT

CHAPTER 42
CALLING OFF THE DOGS

A few days later, Henry the Musician got a return call from his injured friend Esker. "I just heard from the boss man. You finding that famous egg has caused quite an international commotion. The dogs have been called off. Popov hired them through someone named Shamrock. They were already in the area looking for the truck hijackers. Popov had tracked Irv down through a telephone number the Memphis undertaker had found in Marvin Fant's wallet. No telling how he was able to obtain it. Irv won't be bothered any more. The Russian collector wants to make a private offer. He has bought other eggs in the past and wants to present his collection to the foremost museum in Russia. He wasn't happy when he was informed that you have employed a Memphis law firm to take bids for the egg."

Henry emitted a sigh of relief, "Any news about the cereal box money?"

"Yeah. Feelers were put out. Apparently, the money belongs to a crime syndicate on the Gulf Coast. They had a truckload of cash stolen from them. They now know who made the heist, but that fellow is in the pen and has the bulk of it hidden. Their plans are to get to him from the inside and make him squeal."

Henry recalled his prison days. He could imagine the pressure that would drop on poor Shifty.

Esker continued, "The cereal box money from the bank vault is being returned, but I'm to get my cut for being loyal. Thanks a lot, pal."

"You got it."

Henry had chosen the Memphis law firm of Ricks, Tyson, Tinsley, and Arnoff to broker the sale of his Imperial egg. He and Leduc met with Ken Arnoff, a senior partner. Ken's firm had successfully defended the local Merci Hospital in Cade County in a will contest the year before. Ken was introduced to Henry after the trial because Henry had a finder's fee from a devisee's share of the estate.

Ken thought Henry and Leduc were in for a humdrum matter and met with them on a bleak, rainy day in his corner office overlooking Poplar Avenue in East Memphis.

Unidentified sounds came from his mouth when he was shown the photographs of the 1886 Imperial egg and as he absorbed the narrative of Albert Peacock's story.

Ken had his secretary send in Ernest Tinsley, another senior partner in the firm. Ernest gasped upon seeing the pictures. Ken hurriedly called in other associates and secretaries to plan a course of action to sell the egg. Soon the office was overflowing.

A new attorney in the firm suggested, "Why don't we take sealed bids?"

Ken stared. "No way! This is a rare find. We'll put it up for auction and use a premier auction house in New York City."

Ernest interjected, "I'll say the auction will weed out the cheapos and they'll add a buyer's premium to the bid for their fee."

Nods came from the other firm members.

Ken said, "We will have to get the egg authenticated and obtain the proper documentation that certifies that the nephew of Marvin Fant is the owner."

Henry said, "Also, bind down my shared ownership agreement with Rocky Rossi."

Ken laughed. "Hell, yes! That's the basis for our forthcoming fee."

Ernest rubbed his hands gleefully. "I see it coming. Our firm will have worldwide publicity when we announce this discovery and that we are brokering the sale!" he almost shouted.

Ken said, "That's on top of our winning that will contest in Cade County last year. We had to expand our firm because of our exposure from the case."

"This egg won't bring in as much as we got in that case."

Ken smirked. "To be country, I'll say we ain't lettin' this one go!"

CHAPTER 43
THE AUCTION

Henry the Musician and Leduc traveled west on Poplar to Leduc's shop in downtown Memphis. In the back office they discussed the upcoming auction.

Henry remarked thoughtfully, "I think we need to hedge our bets to get the maximum bid on the egg."

"That's what I was thinking," replied Leduc. "What can we do?"

"At my age, this may be my last go-round, my ticket out of the ghetto," said Henry.

"And make all your alimony payments more comfortable?" quipped Leduc.

"I need to find a deep-pocket backer to attend the auction and run the bids up."

"That'll cost us."

"Why don't we decide on what we would take on a straight sale? Then offer the backer a split on the difference up to the high bid," suggested Henry.

"I'll go for that!" grinned Leduc as he rubbed his hands together.

"Since that egg found by the junk dealer brought 30 million, we could use that as a base price and split any excess,"

DRIVER'S FLAT

offered Henry.

"That's a deal. You make the arrangements," agreed Leduc.

Leduc left the office to wait on a customer up front. Henry called a long-distance number from memory. The person he reached was interested immediately. When Henry explained his scheme, the voice replied, "Give me an hour. Wait there."

Two hours later, the call was returned.

"Buddy, you've got a deal. I had to take on two partners to be able to handle a buy this large. We have to remain in the dark on this one. We can give some poor sucker a run for his money. One partner said even if we got stuck with the egg, he would pay us off. He has a new girlfriend he needs to impress," smugly replied the voice.

"Thanks, Trap ..."

"Shhh!" cautioned the voice.

Henry laughed, "Hey, man, the old days are gone! I knew I could count on you."

"We will get back with you later. We have to select a front man to appear and bid. Someone who can't be connected to us."

A few days later a follow-up call was made to Henry with a plan and instructions.

"We have our man. It would be good if we had a gorgeous female companion at the auction for a diversion. Don't you have connections in that category?"

Henry chuckled. "The best one we could find is here in my town. I'll take care of that."

Henry called thirty-year-old Norma Sue Riley, who owned the beauty shop above Potshot's Poolroom, and said, "I need your help."

"Why? How? Why didn't you drop by? Are you afraid of me?" chided Norma Sue.

Henry reddened. She was so pretty that men were intimidated by her.

Henry told about the upcoming auction in New York City and explained what he wanted her to do: show up, look pretty, and be a distraction to other bidders.

"Henry, I can do that better than anybody. What's in it for me? I don't come cheap," needled Norma Sue.

"I was afraid of that. What else do you need besides your pay?"

"I've been to New York City several times. I want to stay at the Four Seasons. And a trip to a top nail salon in Manhattan."

"I guess you're gonna get a watermelon design on your toes?" chimed Henry.

"No, baby. That's too country. But I need to have my hair done at the best shop in town."

"I thought you did hair. Why should I pay for that?"

"I don't do mine."

"Okay. I'll cover all that."

Norma Sue teased, "Will we be sharing a room, baby?"

Henry stuttered, "Uh, no...."

"Why not?"

"I'm not going. I don't fly."

Norma Sue became flirty. "You don't know what you'll be missing: a chance to parade me down a busy sidewalk on your arm in Manhattan and watch other men gawk and fall over themselves. Am I making you blush, baby?"

Henry admitted, "Yes. No other woman can do this to me. I wish I were single again."

"Well, you're not too old for me, but I'm way too young for you. So let's keep our relationship on a business level," laughed Norma Sue.

———

DRIVER'S FLAT

A few weeks later, Ken Arnoff and Ernest Tinsley walked into the auction room of Antonio's Auction House on the seventh floor of a tall building in Manhattan. They had been there several times in the past representing an art gallery in Memphis. They signed the visitor sheet and took seats in a back corner. Although they were several hours early, the room was nearly full. The lawyers knew most in the room were spectators and not bidders. Serious buyers preferred to bid by telephone to remain anonymous. The auction house was not required to announce the identity of a successful bidder, even to the seller.

A young woman, wearing tight jeans and a black beret at a slight angle atop her pretty brunette hair, marched down the aisle amid stares. Her red paisley blouse was open enough to reveal the top of her 36-23-36 figure. She carried herself in complete, unabashed confidence. A murmur came from a group of young executives in the middle of the room. They had never seen a more beautiful woman.

She proceeded to the front, presented her letter of credit, and was given a numbered bidder's paddle. She took a reserved seat on the end of the third row.

Ken Arnoff and Ernest Tinsley stared. They recognized her as one of their witnesses in the Cade County will contest. Norma Sue Riley. They became suspicious. What was she doing here?

The door opened noisily. A slightly tipsy, heavy-set man, dressed in western clothes and a large white Stetson hat, entered. He addressed the room in a loud voice, "I'm Ray Bob Leach from Texas. I've got plenty of oil money, and I aim to spend whatever it takes to bring that 'lil ole play-pretty in that case up there back home to my little granddaughter!" Ray Bob turned and took a long drag from an engraved silver flask he had fished from his jacket pocket. Ray Bob waved at those seated on each side of the aisle as he proceeded to the table up front to present his bank's letter of credit to the auction staff.

"This here ought to be enough to buy that gold trinket. If it ain't, there's more where this came from," bellowed Ray Bob as he plunked the letter on the green blotter. He took his reserved seat on the front row.

The auction staff examined the letter of credit. A clerk whispered to the auction manager, "Wow! Do you think he will bid this much?"

The manager, Ronnie Rivers, gasped when he saw the amount. He became uneasy. He told the clerks he was going to call the bank which was located in Dallas, Texas. Kemp Poe, the bank officer who had signed the letter, was put on the line. The auction manager identified himself and disclosed the nature of his inquiry. He questioned the amount of credit the bank had given Ray Bob.

Kemp verified the amount. "He is one of my bank's major customers but not the best. Generally he is obnoxious and reminds us on every visit of how much money he has and of his self-perceived importance."

"How did he get his money?"

"Oddly enough, he made it through the years by making shrewd deals. He inherited seed money from an uncle. Instead of squandering it and ending up picking oranges in Florida before he was thirty, he parlayed it into a fortune."

Kemp added, "Actually, he has more credit than what was approved."

"Oh?"

"Yeah. Two weeks ago, my bank got two wires to his account. One was from New Orleans, and one was from overseas. They all add up to quite a bit more than what you see. He's stout."

"Thank you, sir. I'm satisfied."

"I'm glad you have to put up with him today instead of me. You'll earn your pay."

There were a number of items to be sold this day besides the Imperial egg. The preview period had not ended when Norma Sue arrived. She left her seat and immediately began examining the auction items. Although none of the young men in the room had yet examined them, each man in the room paraded to the front under the pretense of inspecting the items on sale. Some, more than once. Each eyeballed Norma Sue at length as they returned to their seats. Each received a sweet smile from her.

The auctioneer, slender Benson Bell, who had attended the University of Oxford, struck a gong positioned on the auction block signaling the start of the auction. He spoke with a clipped English accent. He announced the auction rules. Then he began to sell each item.

At the end of the morning, the egg was presented for bids. When Benson Bell finished his description of the egg and its provenance, and that it would be sold without a reserve amount, he asked the room, "Do I have…"

He was interrupted by Norma Sue Riley, who stood and asked, "Can I get another number? I don't like the one I have. I'm bidding for my Sugah Daddy, and his lucky number is seven."

Benson cleared his throat before he announced, "That's an unusual request. The auction has already started, and someone else has been assigned that number."

A young man across the room quickly volunteered, "I have number seven, but I don't need it anymore because I bought the gold cane I wanted. The lady can have my number."

Norma Sue cooed, "Oh, thank you," and sashayed across the room to him unconcerned about the attention her movements attracted.

She exchanged bid paddles with the young man and kissed him on the cheek. The room applauded. The young man later declared he didn't wash his face for a month!

Benson opened the bidding by asking for thirty million. Ray Bob Leach hollered, "Thirty-five!" A telephone bid quickly moved the price to forty. The auctioneer was startled. He had expected to ask for bids in single million dollar increments! Ray Bob stood up and asked rashly, "I want to know who is bidding against me!"

The auctioneer scolded, "Sir, the identity of your opponent does not have to be disclosed. Please, sit down."

The bidding resumed. Ray Bob took a long swig from his flask and boomed, "Sixty! Put that in your pipe and smoke it, Mr. Unknown Big Shot." The onlookers collectively laughed. Benson Bell thought, "How uncouth!"

The telephone bidder responded with a bid for seventy million. Ray Bob bumped the bid by five million. Benson announced to Ray Bob, "Sir, that bid matches your letter of credit amount. That is the last bid I can accept from you." The room filled with applause.

Smelling victory, the telephone bidder came back with seventy-six.

The auctioneer asked for seventy-seven. Silence. He said, "Going once, going twice, going...

"Eighty million," was heard from a sexy voice on the third row. The number seven paddle was seen fanning in the air, gently tossing Norma Sue's tresses.

The auctioneer was shocked! He had assumed that Norma Sue was there to bid on a vintage Patek Philippe watch to be sold later. The auction manager, Ronnie Rivers, immediately took a second look at her letter of credit. It was from the same bank in Dallas as Ray Bob's, but for a much larger amount. It had been signed by a different officer, and there was a notation that it had been verified by the auction house staff. Ronnie smelled collusion between the two to run the bids up. Were they shills for the egg's owner? A good plan, the manager thought, because if the telephone bidder dropped out the owners would only be hung for the auction house commission. The odds were in their favor because only he knew that the anonymous bidder was backed by the budget of an entire country. Ronnie nodded to the auctioneer to proceed.

The telephone bidder responded with ninety, quickly followed by Norma Sue's one hundred and five. The telephone bidder delayed before bidding one hundred and ten. Norma Sue read the hesitation and the reduction in the previous bid premium as a sign of weakness. Benson Bell looked at her with arched eyebrows. Norma Sue turned toward Ray Bob Leach, who had left his seat and was standing in the back corner of the room. With a sober look on his face, he sliced his hand underneath his chin. Norma Sue turned back to the auctioneer and commented, "I'm out. Now my Sugah Daddy has more money to spend on me!"

The Imperial egg was sold for one hundred ten million dollars, with an added buyer's commission.

DRIVER'S FLAT

CHAPTER 44
THE CHECK

A few weeks later, Ken Arnoff's secretary cheerfully called Henry the Musician. She said sweetly, "Mr. Henry, we have a joint check to you and Mr. Rocky Rossi for the sum of fifty-nine million dollars."

Her law firm had successfully negotiated with the auction house to earn their commission by way of a buyer's premium of twenty percent added to the bid amount. The firm received a commission of ten percent from Henry. The firm was holding forty million in escrow for Henry and Leduc's backer.

The secretary was baffled when Henry said nonchalantly, "Just put it in the mail. I'm too busy with my rental houses to run to Memphis right now."

She reported the remark to Ken, who chuckled, "I'll run it down. Call him back and have him meet me in Archie Baker's office tomorrow."

When Ken walked into Archie's office, he found Henry there, along with Chief Deputy Wade Sumrall. Ken had split checks, one for Henry and one for Rocky Rossi.

He asked, "Where did y'all find that egg? Come on, boys. Tell me."

Henry gave him a skimpy description of his quest for the egg up to the point when he and Wade visited Irv. Ken didn't need to know about his contacts and what all was involved in the search.

"So, Irv said Marvin obtained the egg by trading a Rolex watch to an old seaman?"

"Yeah," replied Henry.

"How did the seaman get it?"

"Irv told us what Marvin told him. But we would need Irv's permission to pass it on."

"Could y'all visit him? Historians around the world would be interested to know how it got from the Imperial Palace to a chicken house."

"We'll do that and give you a report."

As Ken left, he smiled. "I can't believe that a long sought-after piece of art worth millions has been stored in a barrel of peanuts in a miser's chicken house for thirty years!"

Wade laughed. "Now I understand why a banty rooster was so irate when Henry and I entered the chicken pen. He was guarding his lady, the most beautiful hen in the world!"

DRIVER'S FLAT

CHAPTER 45
ED

Sheriff Grady Powers finally followed up on Burl's earlier tip from the poolroom at Baxter and Clytee's remark to Wade at Lola's. He dropped by Ed's junkyard on the highway near Vena. It was a sprawling salvage yard surrounded by a high chain-link fence with barbed wire on top. The yard was filled with inoperable vehicles of all sizes and ages. Grady parked in front of the small office that sat by a locked double gate. As he walked past the back end of a used Nissan car, he did a double take. His trained eyes noticed the broken glass on the left taillight.

Inside, Ed was talking to a customer who was dressed in greasy overalls. Ed was a skinny, sandy-haired man, about sixty years old. He had the stub of a Tampa Nugget cigar clamped in one side of his mouth. The junkyard was one of his many business ventures. Ed had a nose for identifying money-making projects. In the past, he had owned a body shop, a mobile home lot, a furniture factory, and a motel. He also had an uncanny aptitude to leave a business just before its market dropped.

Ed and the customer were haggling over the price of a transmission still attached to a 1957 Chevy parked near the end

DRIVER'S FLAT

of one line of junk vehicles inside the fence. Grady stood to one side and smiled to himself as he gazed out the picture window of the office.

Ed said, "I'll take $50."

The customer gawked! He knew it was worth $200. He hurriedly said, "I'll take it."

"There's a retrieval fee of $100," added Ed.

"Ain't that a lot?" asked the customer.

"Well, you can go get it yourself," replied Ed.

Grady chuckled at the conversation. Ed had a foolproof security system. When he first bought the salvage yard, he was robbed blind on weekends by burglars. Ed liked to party in Memphis, and his favorite club was the Crimson Feather. At noon every Saturday, Ed closed the yard. He and his wife would travel to Memphis in his motorhome to party with friends. This regular habit was noticed by local parts thieves, and they helped themselves while Ed was away.

Ed was a stubborn fellow and would go to extremes not to be outdone by an adversary. None of the security devices he had placed at the yard had been successful. One night at the Crimson Feather club, several friends were listening to his incessant whining about the raids on his yard. An ex-con, sitting at Ed's table, clued him in on how to stop the break-ins. Ed acted on the advice the next week and had the system in place by the time he left for Memphis on Saturday.

Eagerly, Ed got up early on Monday morning and arrived at the salvage yard gates just after daylight to see if the trap had worked. He heard screams near an old truck parked midway in one of the vehicle lines. He moved down the fence where he had a clear view of the adjoining lanes. He quickly dialed 911. Deputy Sheriff Hampton soon arrived and got into the company pickup with Ed, who drove toward the sounds. An unconscious young man who was still holding on to a wrench was on the ground by the old truck. Wade immediately recognized him as a local thief with a long rap sheet who went by the alias, "Sparkplug."

The screams could be heard coming from underneath the truck. Furiously pawing the ground near the running board of the vehicle stood Ed's security system: a seven-foot-tall ostrich! As Ed led the bird away with a bucket of feed, the other thief, with the alias, "Carburetor," crawled out.

Later, the two told Wade that they went through the yard fence before daybreak. They had just started removing a part from the vehicle when they heard a booming sound. They looked up to see a weird, flat head on top of a long neck. They froze, giving the male ostrich the opportunity to kick Sparkplug unconscious. Carburetor dived underneath the truck for safety. He was terrified because he had never seen even a picture of this kind of bird, a bird that was trying to scratch him out.

Word of the incident quickly spread, and Ed had no more thefts. Not to let a dollar pass him by, he later bought a female to mate with his guard bird. Ed advertised her fruit as "Ostrich egg. $500. As is, where is."

The customer recalled hearing about Ed's security system. He agreed to the retrieval fee. He waited outside while one of Ed's helpers went for the part.

Ed winked at Wade, who asked, "Does the sum of $19,900 mean anything to you?"

Ed refused to look at Wade as he replied, "Possibly."

His posture and answer assured Wade that it did and that Ed probably was involved.

He knew he had hit paydirt when Ed asked, "All in one wad, or scattered?"

"Maybe both... at one time, or another."

Then Ed subjected Wade to some of his doublespeak, for which he was known.

"Just say that a man had a deal lined up to make some money. But he had to go and stay somewhere for months. And while he was gone, another man, who found out about the deal, moved in and captured the profit while nothing could be done about it."

"Was the first man's vacation free?" asked Wade.

"Yeah. Those kinds are always free, but you don't have a choice of your destination."

"Has the first man had that kind of vacation before?"

"Yep. Several of them."

The pen, thought Wade. I knew the Musician was involved. He asked, "What was the profit on the deal?"

"$19,900," replied Ed. He continued, "Suppose the first man had a friend who had an order for a special part for an old dump truck. And suppose the friend knew where a disabled one was on the side of a road. Suppose the friend went to check out the truck and discovered its bed was full of money."

"Okay," said Wade. He was beginning to see where this was going. He was confident he was talking to "the friend."

"Suppose the friend knew who owned the old truck and told the first man. And the friend was aware that a shipment of drug money had been stolen."

"Go on."

"Suppose the first man told his friend how much to take, but leave the rest in case the second man's theft was discovered. The second man might have to pay the full amount back, or else."

"Sounds like a message."

"Two. The exact amount of money to be taken, with the rest not to be bothered, was the first one."

"What was the second?"

"The friend was told to scatter the new money in public so the second man would hear about it. The second man couldn't come forward and make a claim because he had stolen it in the first place."

Wade laughed.

Ed said, "The coffee shop crowds have been tracking the amounts found and came up with a total of around $13,900."

"That's how much we are holding. There's still $6,000 not been reported."

"It won't be."

"Why?"

Ed grinned. "That would be the cost of an aerial surveillance of a loading barn and handling charges. That friend would have put in a lot of effort, with the help of a couple of sidekicks, to strew the money at that many locations and not be spotted."

Wade mused, "I wonder why the 'friend' didn't help himself from the stash?"

Ed winked. "Because the first man told him a hit was out on the thief, and I didn't want to be added to the list!"

When Wade got back to the office, he called Tina, the county attorney, and reported what Ed had told him.

She laughed. "Giving away stolen money might be a crime, but do you think Ed would testify about the first man?"

"Nope."

"Well, return all the money you're holding to the finders."

"Does that include the Lucky Charms money?"

"Yeah. The syndicate is not in a position to come forth with a claim."

"That's good. Little Mollie Carver and her mother sure could use it."

Tina said, "I agree. I bet Lucky Charms will always be their cereal!"

DRIVER'S FLAT

CHAPTER 46
AFTERMATH

Henry's telephone was ringing incessantly. He was in a sullen mood and wouldn't answer. He was disgusted about how his lifestyle had been ruined when the news broke about his windfall from the auction. Henry had worked hard to retain a mysterious persona.

He was baffled as to how he had been identified as the Imperial egg's owner. The auction house had agreed not to disclose him as the seller. When he questioned them about this issue, they assured him the Antonio Auction House had remained confidential. So who had blabbed?

All his ex-wives called, just like they were still married to him. Each, in turn, refused to hear him say no to their money requests. Cousins he didn't know he had sent him letters asking for financial help for skeptical business ventures. He couldn't get out of his driveway most days because of a rabble of freeloaders clamoring for money. He had lived around the corner from Elvis in Memphis for years and didn't recall the king having to deal with this much turmoil.

Henry had whined to his friend Deputy Hampton. Wade asked if he and Loophole Lawrence were friends.

DRIVER'S FLAT

"Yes. We go back a long ways. Loophole represented me at my first parole revocation hearing. We're tight."

Wade suggested, "Make a $10 donation to a distant charity. Have Loophole draft a letter from you to the public that you donated your egg money to charity. Publish it in the newspaper. Loophole is crafty. He should be able to make the letter sound like you donated 'All' your money. That should get those parasites off your back."

The phone stopped ringing after the third tone. Then it rang again three times. Henry brightened. That was a signal that Leduc was calling.

Henry picked up the receiver and spoke, "What's happening?"

"The Imperial egg went home to Russia," answered Leduc.

"How do you know?"

"Before the artifact was returned to Russia, the owner's operatives brought it to Albert Peacock for some cosmetic restoration. Popov met them at Albert's shop and surveilled his repair. When the Russians left with the egg for the airport, Popov wandered up the street to my shop.

"According to Popov, the mysterious telephone bidder at the auction was the wealthy Russian businessman who already owns two of the Imperial eggs. He is very angry at our ploy to rig the bids. He figured out how he was set up. He was forced to bid way more than he had planned."

Henry laughed with glee, "I learned how to work bids from a former cellmate! My lessons paid off."

Leduc reasoned, "Popov was able to identify us as the responsible parties. Per vengeful instructions from his boss, Popov let the news leak to the public so our new riches would be accompanied with lifelong misery."

DRIVER'S FLAT

"He succeeded at that," ruefully acknowledged Henry, wishing he had never found the treasure. He needed to call Trudy for the address of her hiding place.

ACKNOWLEDGEMENTS

To: My office staff, Amy Harmon and Alicia Havens for their support in getting the book to print.

I'm forever grateful to my friend Forrest H. "Popie" Pope for his willingness to revisit his inexhaustible cache of memories of Memphis nightlife and the transgressions of Southern criminals.

Thanks to Rex Sanderson and Leland Norman, Jr. for sharing information about the hitchhiker.

ABOUT THE AUTHOR

Sonny Clanton is the author of *Mr. Joab's Will*, a legal thriller. He lives in Calhoun City, Mississippi, located on the eastern end of Grenada Lake.